"A woma...
beauty sh...
for her ...
the depth of her mind, as well."

Sighing inwardly, she fought against the smile tickling the corners of her lips.

Santiago was more eloquent than an eighteenth-century poet, and his words were filled with such tender warmth that they resonated in her soul. It was the sweetest thing anyone had ever said to her, and to her surprise, she believed every word. "I don't know what to say."

"Then don't say anything." His eyes smiled, swept over her like the gentle breeze ruffling the curtains. "Call me whenever you need to talk or vent about how unfair life is. I've been there, and I know how important it is to have someone in your corner."

Sparks flew when he clasped her hand.

"Thank you, Santiago. I just might take you up on that offer."

"I hope you do...."

His mouth was less than an inch away—poised, ready, waiting.

Their lips crushed together. Moved hungrily over each other with the same urgency as their roving hands.

The kiss was ferocious.

Explosive.

So devastating she'd need weeks to recover from it.

PAMELA YAYE

has a bachelor's degree in Christian education and has been writing short stories since elementary school. Her love for African-American fiction and literature prompted her to actively pursue a career in writing romance. When she's not reading or working on her latest novel, she's watching basketball, cooking or planning her next vacation. Pamela lives in Calgary, Canada, with her handsome husband and adorable daughter.

Escape
to
PARADISE

PAMELA YAYE

KIMANI
ROMANCE

I can hardly believe that this is my tenth Kimani Romance novel.
It seems like just yesterday I sat down at the computer and
started typing out the sexy love story running through my mind.
I feel so blessed, and fortunate to have such a wonderful, supportive
family. You guys are the best thing that has ever happened to me,
and I adore every one of you. I love you Yaye's and Odidison's!!!

Sha-Shana (of Sha-Shana Crichton & Associates) I still remember
the day you called and offered to represent me. I was big, and pregnant,
but I jumped like ten feet in the air! Ha,ha I hope our future is filled
with more contracts, proposals and a trip somewhere warm and tropical
with men who look and smell like Santiago Medina!

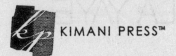

KIMANI PRESS™

Recycling programs
for this product may
not exist in your area.

ISBN-13: 978-0-373-86246-7

ESCAPE TO PARADISE

Dear Reader,

Ever wish you could get away from it all? Your job, your family, the world spinning out of control around you? That's exactly how Claudia Jeffries feels! When her ex-husband is arrested on eight counts of corporate fraud the same day their divorce is finalized, the media spotlight blares brightly on her. A confrontation with an enraged investor leaves Claudia shaken and scared and desperate to clear her name. Overwhelmed by all of the unwanted attention, Claudia decides to leave town until the story dies down. Goodbye, Richmond; Hello, Cabo San Lucas, Mexico! "Leave everything behind" is the slogan of the Sea of Cortez Resort, and when Claudia arrives at her secluded condo nestled among lush palm trees and tropical flowers, she feels the stress of the past month begin to melt away.

Santiago Medina *can't* stop staring at the radiant, toffee-skinned beauty standing in the lobby of his family's resort. He's never been this drawn to anyone and, when he discovers it's the same woman who shot him down in the luxury airport lounge hours earlier, he sets out to show the Southern beauty there's more to him than meets the eye. Luckily for Claudia, Santiago doesn't scare easily or believe in giving up without a fight....

Escape to Paradise is my tenth Kimani Romance novel, and in honor of its release, I will be running contests on my website all month long. To find out more about me and my novels, and enter to win a super-cool prize pack, visit me at www.pamelayaye.com.

With love,

Pamela Yaye

Chapter 1

I can't believe I'm sneaking out of my own house, Claudia Jefferies thought, pitching her pink travel bag through the second-story window of her quaint brick home nestled in the heart of downtown Richmond. *But what choice do I have? I either skip town until the story dies down or live in constant fear.*

Before second thoughts set in, she gathered her courage and jumped. Claudia landed in the flower bed, but instantly sprang to her feet. And her sister said she needed to go on a diet! *Humpf.* If not for the soft cushion padding her stomach she would have broken her ribs.

Moving swiftly, she cleaned the dirt off her clothes, retrieved the bag and climbed over her neighbor's fence. She had to hurry, or she was going to be late to meet Max. The sun crept over the horizon, turning the sky a pinkish-orange hue. Like her, the night was making a hasty retreat, falling to the shadows like the leaves sailing to the ground.

Feeling a chill in the autumn wind, Claudia pulled her

cashmere scarf tightly across her shoulders. Cold singed her ears, reminding her of the drastic measures she'd taken last night to conceal her identity. Against the advice of her sister, she'd driven to a neighborhood dubbed the Devil's Playground and found a small, out-of-the-way beauty salon. Once seated in the vinyl chair, she'd ordered the gum-popping stylist to "chop it all off and dye it black." The young woman stared at her as if she'd just confessed to committing double murder. Surprise pinched her plump face, and her pierced tongue lay limp in her mouth.

"Is there a problem?" Claudia asked, shifting uncomfortably in her chair. Did the woman recognize her? Was that why she was copping an attitude?

"Don't do this, ma'am. He's not worth it."

Now, Claudia was the one with wrinkled brows and puckered lips. The stylist wasn't making any sense, and she was so loud she'd attracted the attention of the entire salon. "I don't understand," she whispered, hoping the woman would follow her lead and lower her voice. "Who's not worth what?"

"Sisters storm in here every day demanding I chop their hair off, only to regret it when they reunite with their boyfriends a week later."

"Well, I'm not one of them. I'd sooner become a lesbian than take my ex back."

The stylist drew her fingers through Claudia's lush brown locks. "Are you sure about this? Normally I wouldn't dissuade a client from trying something new, but you have the kind of hair most women dream of! It's long and thick and full of body."

"I'm sure, and if you finish within the hour, I'll give you a *very* generous tip." Claudia patted her purse as if it was stuffed with hundred-dollar bills. "Please hurry, I'm in a rush."

That was all it took.

Forty-five minutes later, Claudia sailed out of the beauty

salon feeling like a younger, trendier version of her thirty-year-old self. Angled bangs fell dramatically across her right eye, thick layers kissed the tips of her ears and the sleek, black hue gave her a bold, bad-girl edge.

Touching her fingertips to the nape of her neck, Claudia wondered if she'd ever get used to the chic, no-fuss do. Unrecognizable now, she loved the anonymity that her new look provided and planned to use it to her advantage. That was why she was making a run for it while she still had the chance.

With fast, quick steps, she hustled down the alley, toward the city center. Another block and she'd be in the clear, home free. But instead of shooting across the intersection, she paused at the top of her street.

Reporters, clutching coffee cups and microphones, were camped out on her lawn like a bunch of well-dressed vultures. They were peering into her windows and trampling through her garden to set up camera equipment. Spotting her favorite reporter—a woman who took on only the meatiest news stories—reminded Claudia of just how serious the situation was. Anger welled up inside her, but she swallowed hard and gathered herself. Claudia never imagined that she'd be the lead story on the evening news, and as she considered the events of the last two weeks she cursed the day she'd laid eyes on William Prescott III.

Shivering like a naked woman sleeping on a park bench, Claudia stuck her hands into her pockets and resumed walking, her thoughts on the man she'd been married to for the better part of a decade. Disgust churned in her stomach at the thought of her heartless ex-husband.

The night they met played in Claudia's mind like a movie on the big screen. When William Prescott, CEO of the largest investment firm in the South, approached her at a bar mitzvah she'd been hired to plan, Claudia wasn't sure what to make of him. The suave, brown-eyed businessman had a reputation with the ladies, and after he introduced himself she could see why. He was forward, the type of guy who wouldn't take no for an answer, and although he was too aggressive for her tastes, she admired his self-confidence. He was ten years her senior, but after dating a string of immature boys, she welcomed being with a strong, take-charge man. Dating a man of William's stature opened doors for her, and when they married after a brief, whirlwind courtship, the city's elite had come calling.

Her event-planning business, Signature Party Planners, took off like a rocket, netting six-figure profits that year, but her life was far from perfect.

Shaking off bitter memories, she turned onto Atwell Avenue. Anxious to put more distance between herself and the media hounds, Claudia hustled across the street as if her life depended on it. And it did. The sooner she got out of Richmond the better.

A black Honda Civic with personalized plates was idling at the curb. Her heart pounded, beating strong and fast. Approaching the car, she glanced cautiously over her shoulder. Claudia didn't see anyone, but that didn't mean no one was watching. Opening the back door, she slipped inside and dropped her bags at her feet.

"You weren't kidding about wanting a drastic change," Maxine said, turning around to face her. "I almost didn't recognize you! Cutting your hair short was a good move, sis."

"Let's get going. I don't want to attract any attention."

A scowl pinched her scarlet-red lips. Ghetto chic, and proud of it, her older sister could give an exotic dancer half her age a serious run for her money. "This is not a shuttle service and I'm certainly not a cabbie, so get up front."

"Just drive. I'll explain later."

"I don't even know where we're going."

"The airport."

"The airport!" she yelled, her eyes shooting out of her head. "Where are you going?"

"I'm not sure yet. I just need to get out of town." Peering outside the window, she clicked on her seat belt and slid down in her seat. "Someone might be tailing us, so be on guard. Reporters are very crafty, and they'll do just about anything to get a story."

"You've been watching too much *TMZ!*" Laughing, Maxine put the car in Drive and joined the light, early-morning traffic. "Are the reporters still camped outside of your house?"

"There were more pulling up as I left."

"Keep your chin up, sis. I know the last few weeks have been tough, but hang in there."

"'Tough' is an understatement. Since the arrest my life has become a living hell."

"Oh, come on. Things aren't that bad."

"You're right. They're worse." To keep from having another breakdown, Claudia slowly drew air in and out of her lungs.

How could something like this happen to someone like me? she wondered, fighting back tears. She'd done everything the right way. Gone to university. Graduated with honors. Worked tirelessly to build her event-planning business. But it was her desire to have a family of her own that had been her downfall. And so she'd overlooked William's selfish ways and stayed in the marriage as long as she did. "I woke up this morning thinking the last few days were a bad dream, but then the phone started ringing and I remembered how many lives William destroyed, how many people he's hurt."

"Is that why you called and asked me to meet you here?"

Afraid she'd dissolve into tears if she spoke, she nodded in response.

"The story will die down before you know it." Maxine watched her kid sister in the rearview mirror. "You've been through far worse and survived, so try not to stress."

Claudia drew strength from her sister's words. She'd come

a long way, overcome insurmountable odds. It was a miracle she'd made it out of Lynchburg's eight-block housing project in one piece, but despite all the hard times, she knew growing up in the hood had made her who she was today—a tough, hard-nosed woman who wasn't afraid to fight.

If that's true, her conscience challenged, *then why are you running away?*

Because what happened last night terrified me.

"I thought I was strong enough to handle all of the media attention," she began, shuddering at the thought of what had taken place twenty-four hours earlier, "but it's become too much. The prank calls, the cruel stares I get whenever I'm out in public."

"The chatter will die down before you know it."

Claudia wasn't so confident. Not after everything that had happened since her ex-husband's arrest. Her mind slipped back to two weeks earlier, to the day her peaceful, uneventful life took a turn for the worst. She woke up that morning with a smile on her face, a song in her heart and a reason to celebrate. Finally, after months of William's bitching and complaining, their divorce was final. He was gone, out of her life forever.

Or so she thought.

Shaking her head, she remembered the exact moment her world came crashing down around her. The phone rang, and a husky voice on the other end asked her to comment on William's arrest. Claudia hung up the phone. It had to be a prank call. A bunch of bored suburban kids who had nothing better to do than play phone games. But the calls kept coming. The *Wall Street Journal. Newsday.* Her friends and associates. It seemed everyone knew the details of the case except her.

Their questions were harsh, probing. And filled in the missing pieces of the puzzle. Her ex-husband and three of his business partners had been indicted on eight counts of corporate fraud. Logging on to the computer confirmed it, and the pounding in her head—that started seconds after the first phone call—quickly infected the rest of her body. The whole city was talking about the collapse of Qwest Capital Investments, and Claudia couldn't turn on the television without seeing another interview with a teary, shell-shocked investor. Her heart went out to each and every one of them, from the retired naval officer to the school superintendent.

Claudia didn't know what to believe, and everything she read bordered on lunacy. She was stunned by the arrest, absolutely blindsided by it. William was a lot of things, but he wasn't a crook, was he? The question ran through her mind again when the two plainclothes detectives arrived later that day to interview her.

Or rather, to interrogate her.

They questioned her about William's business dealings and eyed her suspiciously when she didn't give them the answers they were looking for. Then, after an hour in the hot seat, they accused her of being his accomplice. Burning with indignation, she vehemently denied the accusation. The detectives were convinced she was lying and threatened to haul her down to the precinct for further questioning. Images of being handcuffed, booked and fingerprinted attacked her mind. What would her clients think if she was named as a coconspirator in the case? And how would it affect her company? When it was all said and done, would she even *have* a business to worry about?

Claudia cleared all thoughts of her ex-husband and his troubles from her mind. Like she'd told the two detectives who'd interviewed her, William wasn't her problem anymore, and she had better things to do than waste time pondering his guilt or innocence.

"How long will you be gone?"

"I'm not sure. A month. Maybe longer. It all depends on how things play out. I was thinking of going to Lynchburg to see Aunt Hattie, but I haven't made up my mind yet."

"But the last time you went down there you vowed to never go back."

"I know, but I'm desperate," she admitted. "I haven't done anything wrong, but I'm being made out to be the bad guy. You'd think I was the one who embezzled two million dollars from Qwest Capital Investments."

"The only reason the media's taken an interest in you is because you're the beautiful, much-younger trophy wife." Maxine shrugged and offered a sympathetic smile. "Your rags-to-riches story makes for good TV, and it will probably sell a ton of newspapers, too."

Thinking about the state of her event-planning business made Claudia's hopes crumble and her shoulders sag in despair. "I've lost three jobs in one week."

"You're planning the mayor's luncheon, and that's bound to be great for business."

Claudia cleared her throat. "Someone called yesterday from his office and said my services were no longer needed."

"I don't understand why you're being punished for something William did. *He's* the one who stole from his investors, not you."

The tears Claudia had been holding in finally broke free. "I feel terrible about what he's done," she confessed, covering her face with her hands, "and I can't help feeling responsible. I was his wife. I should have known what he was doing, I should have stopped him."

The car jerked forward violently when Maxine slammed on the brakes.

"Don't you dare blame yourself for what he did," she scolded, twisting around in her seat like a human pretzel. "William ruined those people's lives, not you. You were surprised by his arrest, just like the rest of us."

"I wish there was something I could do to help his victims." Sniffling, Claudia cleaned her mascara-stained cheeks with her fingertips. "If my accounts weren't frozen I'd—"

Maxine gasped. "The banks froze your accounts? They can't do that!"

"They can if there's a court order. The Securities and Exchange Commission filed a request with the court on Monday, and there was nothing my lawyer could do to stop it."

"I don't understand why the authorities are pursuing you. You're innocent."

"The investigators are convinced I was in on it, and since we were married for ten years and only recently divorced, they argued for additional time to substantiate their case against me." Hearing herself repeat her attorney's words made the situation more real, made her realize that things were going to get a whole lot worse before they got better. And that brought a fresh batch of tears. "Mr. Tibbs said I'll probably be subpoenaed to testify in William's case."

"I can't believe these people. Next thing you know they'll be fitting you with an ankle bracelet and confiscating your passport."

"They tried, but the judge refused." Claudia forced a smile. "It's a small victory. At least I'm free to come and go as I please without fear of being hunted down."

"If you need anything, just ask. Money's been tight ever since Royce lost his job, but I don't mind dipping into my savings to help you out."

"I couldn't ask you to do that. You're pregnant."

"I know, but it's the least I could do. I was the one who encouraged you to date William and look how things turned out." Maxine made a clicking sound with her teeth. "If I had known he was a lying scoundrel, I never would have advised you to marry him."

"That's in the past. I've moved on, and despite everything that's going on right now I'm in a really good place." Claudia tugged on her cap, pulling it down so low it covered her eyebrows. Okay, so she was lying, but she didn't want Max to feel guilty about something that wasn't her fault. William was her past, and as of last Thursday they were officially done. That painful chapter of her life was over and she was determined to move on.

To escape the thoughts crowding her mind—thoughts of losing her house, her business and her sanity—Claudia shut her eyes and leaned back in her seat. "I wish I could disappear. Just go somewhere where nobody knows my name."

"Oh, that's right, they don't have TVs or newspapers in Lynchburg," Maxine quipped, her tone ripe with sarcasm. "You know how much Aunt Hattie likes to talk. The whole town will know you're coming before your plane touches down!"

They drove in silence for a moment, and then Maxine let out an ear-piercing shriek. It was so deafening Claudia was surprised the windows didn't shatter into a million pieces.

"You should go to Cabo San Lucas!"

"I can hardly afford the plane ticket to Lynchburg, let alone to Mexico."

Weaving in and out of traffic like a NASCAR driver going for broke, Maxine took the exit marked Departures, zoomed up the ramp and flew into the first available parking space. "Royce and I had such a great time there during our honeymoon that we purchased time shares. It's a good thing we did when the market was strong, because we could never afford it now."

Claudia screwed her face into a frown. "I don't want to go to a resort that's packed with kids and rude tourists. I need to rest, clear my head."

"And you think you can relax in Lynchburg? I love Aunt Hattie but she yaks nonstop. You'd get more peace and quiet staying at an amusement park!"

A giggle tickled the back of Claudia's throat. It didn't matter how bad she felt, Max could always make her laugh. "Don't bad-mouth Aunt Hattie. She's the only family we've got left."

"Then we're in *really* bad shape!"

Claudia didn't laugh, but Maxine did. Her laugh was smooth, easy, as if she didn't have a care in the world. And she didn't. Despite her present financial woes, she had a husband who loved her, a home in a gated community and not a single reporter camped outside her house.

"Picture it," she said, spreading her hands out in front of her. "You stretched out on a beach, sipping cocktails under the hot Mexican sun, and being served fresh fruit by an Antonio Banderas look-alike with rock-hard abs and a tight ass!"

"That's no way for a pregnant woman to talk."

"Girl, please, I'm only a few months along. The babies can't hear anything!"

Claudia shook her head at her sister.

"Go to Cabo and enjoy yourself," Maxine instructed. "I promise you won't be sorry."

Famous for its breathtaking waterfalls and endless blue skies, Cabo San Lucas was reputed to be one of the most beautiful peninsulas on earth and a place Claudia had always wanted to see. But her furious work schedule left few hours to sleep, let alone travel to faraway lands.

"The Sea of Cortez Resort is world-class all the way. I damn near fainted when Royce carried me into our ocean-front suite. And who knows," she said with a devilish smirk, "maybe you'll meet someone while you're down there. A night of passion with a sexy tourist is exactly what your sex-deprived ass needs."

"I'd rather swim in shark-infested waters than indulge in a seedy holiday fling. After everything I've been through, the last thing I want is to get caught up with another no-good man."

"There are still some good guys out there, and it's high time you met somebody new."

"My divorce was only finalized two weeks ago."

"Yeah, but you've been legally separated for a year,"

Maxine challenged, her tone accusatory. "I don't know how you've gone that long without having sex. I need a man to keep me warm at night, or I'll go insane!"

Claudia shrugged, conveying how little she cared about having a man in her bed. Since they were teens, her sister had treated dating like an amateur sport and, if not for getting knocked up by her boyfriend-turned-husband four months ago, she'd still be racking up numbers in her little black book. "Maybe I should go down to Cabo for a few weeks."

"Of course you should!" Maxine nodded her head fervently, as if she was praising a small child. "The suite is in my name, but if you show two forms of ID you should be fine."

"And if that doesn't work?"

Her smile was sly. "Then flash some skin! That always works for me!"

"Could you be serious for one moment? I don't want to fly all the way down to this resort only to be turned away." Annoyed that her sister was making light of her being stranded, she decided to stick to her original plan. "Forget it. I'm going to Lynchburg. I don't need any more stress, and I could see this whole Cabo thing blowing up in my face."

"I'll call the resort to let them know that you're coming. How's that?"

Maxine put the car in Park and hopped out. "I can't wait to hear what you think of the suite, so give me a ring as soon as you get settled."

Claudia didn't know why, but getting out of the car took enormous effort. The strain of the last two weeks had finally caught up to her, and when she stood up she had to grip the door to keep from falling. Her travel bag felt heavy, as if someone had snuck twenty-pound weights inside, but she tossed it over her shoulder and smiled. "Thanks for everything, Max."

"Have a safe trip and try not to worry about all the craziness that's going on down here." Maxine hugged her tight. "You've done nothing wrong, so stop persecuting yourself."

Claudia nodded, told herself that her sister was right, but that didn't stop her from feeling like a fugitive. And when she boarded the United plane bound for Washington, D.C., and saw her ex-husband's picture on the front of the *Richmond Times-Dispatch* newspaper, her fears of being arrested and traipsed in front of the news media returned with a vengeance.

Chapter 2

Santiago Medina didn't make it a habit to stare. Or to approach strangers at the airport, but he couldn't take his eyes off the woman who had just entered the Dulles International Airport first-class lounge. He loved long hair, but her short, trendy hairstyle was stunning. And so were her almond-shaped eyes. They were so bright, so luminous, it was impossible for him to look away. She had to be a dancer, a performer, someone who made a living thrilling audiences on a Las Vegas stage. No way she was stuck behind a desk working a regular nine-to-five. Not with that radiant butterscotch skin, that oval face and those pretty, luscious lips.

His mouth dried, but Santiago doubted that water could quench his thirst. Ridiculously beautiful, she had a unique, ethereal look that made her stand out in the thick crowd of commuters. Her face was free of makeup, scrubbed clean, but her beauty was undeniable. He wanted to touch her. And not just because she had the slender shape of a ballerina and legs that stretched on for miles. He'd always been able to see with his heart what others couldn't see with their eyes, and he sensed that this woman was in enormous pain. Sadness seeped from her pores. It enveloped her, hovered like a ghost. Her grief was palpable, real, so heavy the entire luxury lounge was cloaked in it.

The overhead lights flickered, and for a moment Santiago feared the power would go out. He glanced outside the window and released a heavy sigh. Rain shot down from somber gray clouds, and lightning bathed the sky in a blinding white hue. Thunder boomed, crashed, roared like a train flying down the tracks. His flight to Cabo San Lucas had been delayed—twice—and if the weather advisory for D.C. was lifted in the next twenty-four hours he'd consider it a divine act of God.

Leaning back in his seat, he cleared his mind of all stress, of all worries. He was anxious to see his family, but he couldn't help wondering if the brutal weather was a sign of things to come. Were stormy days ahead? His mother was booked to have abdominal surgery at the end of the month and she would be out of commission for weeks. His workaholic father would rather travel the country brokering new deals than help manage the resort. It was up to him to oversee the renovation project, and he was already dreading every minute of it.

Santiago calculated the number of hours he'd spent waiting at Dulles International Airport and strangled a groan of frustration. He was stranded, but at least he was comfortable. The spacious first-class lounge had all the comforts of home—semireclining chairs, plush oversize couches, and a restaurant that carried everything from crab salad to Peking duck.

He picked up the *Newsweek* magazine lying on the glass table and started to read. Two sentences in, his gaze strayed back across the room. He guessed that she was in her midtwenties, but from ten feet away it was hard to know for sure.

She looked wounded, broken, but she walked into the lounge with unparalleled grace. She moved with poise, confidence, the elegance of an Oscar-winning actress. And when she sat down in his line of vision, only a few rows away from him, he caught a whiff of her fragrant perfume.

Santiago watched her on the sly. Filled with compassion, he wondered why she looked so sad, why she had such a heavy heart. Was she flying home to care for an ailing relative? Or to attend the funeral of a close, dear friend?

Santiago saw a slim man slide up to her. The woman frowned, said a few words he couldn't make out, and resumed staring out the window. Shoulders hunched in defeat, the stranger slunk off alone toward the bar. A second later another guy showed up. He was a dead ringer for 50 Cent, and his jeans were so low he was waddling like a pregnant woman in her last trimester. This time, the woman didn't even turn around. Off the guy went with his tail between his legs. On and on it went until Santiago lost count of her suitors.

Amused, he watched as the woman dissed and dismissed every man who approached her. What was the matter with these guys? Couldn't they see that she was upset? She needed a friend, someone to tell her that God was bigger than her problems. And he was just the man to do it.

Tossing down the magazine, he straightened his shoulders and adjusted his clothes. Opening his carry-on bag, he fished out his favorite cologne and sprayed some on his shirt collar. *Just because I can't take a shower doesn't mean I can't smell nice.* He started his workday as early as six o'clock, sometimes earlier. Before most people got out of bed he had already showered, changed and reviewed the morning's agenda. Being a freelance business consultant was a taxing job, filled with enormous stress and long hours, but he derived great pleasure from fixing companies on the brink of financial ruin. And his six-figure fee wasn't chump change.

Santiago stood, but didn't make any moves toward her.

Second thoughts set in, pelting him in the back like rocks. *You saw what she did to those other guys,* his conscience jeered. *What makes you think she won't humiliate you, too?* He shrugged off his doubts. There was nothing to fear. After all, he wasn't trying to make a love connection. His motives were pure; his desire was to help, to reach out. Two years ago he'd been entrenched in the depths of grief, so consumed with pain he was convinced he'd die of a broken heart. But then he'd had the good fortune of meeting Father Francis, and the Catholic priest had helped restore his faith. That was why he had to reach out to her. *It's my Christian duty,* he told himself, forcing his eyes away from her sinful curves.

Wallet in hand, he strode purposely through the private seating area and joined the line for the snack bar. As Santiago placed his order and then collected the food, he was attacked by a severe case of self-doubt. His limbs felt weak, like they were coated in papier-mâché. He couldn't remember ever being this nervous. Not even when— Santiago steeled himself against those painful memories. He wasn't going there. Not today. He had to move forward, had to keep living. He planned to tell this to the beautiful young woman staring aimlessly out the window. He'd lived through a devastating tragedy, but he was still here. He was still standing.

His confidence came roaring back. *I can do this,* he told himself. *It's no big deal.* But when she glanced his way and their eyes met, Santiago knew his mission was in jeopardy before it had even begun.

Half-dead with exhaustion, Claudia dropped into her seat hungry, tired and shivering with cold. The turbulence on the United flight was so severe, she could hardly think, let alone sleep, and although the Boeing 747 had landed safely at Dulles International Airport, she'd stumbled off the plane feeling more stressed out than ever.

Her stomach grumbled, rumbled like the thunder wreaking havoc outside, but Claudia didn't even consider getting up from her plush chair. Sleep first, food second. Crossing her legs, she nestled her chin inside her sweater and closed her eyes. The darkness provided a reprieve, a much-needed break from her thoughts.

Her mind cleared.

Her breathing slowed.

Her limbs relaxed.

Imagining herself on a white sandy beach, stretched out on a comfy lounge chair, brought an indulgent smile to Claudia's lips. Sunshine rained down from the sky, the wind carried the scent of calla lilies and she could hear the waves lapping softly against—

"It's over. The company's finished."

"You think so?"

"Hell yeah! And the CEO and his bandits are to blame. Damn crooks."

Claudia's eyes flapped open. Her daydream came to a screeching halt, and fear shot through her veins. It was hard to breathe. No, impossible. The men sitting behind her in the first-class lounge were discussing the collapse of Qwest Capital Investments. The news of William's arrest had reached Washington? *Of course it had!* her inner voice screamed. The Dow plunged the day her ex was indicted and, according to published reports, the company had lost millions.

"The wife's definitely in cahoots with him."

"Not necessarily. Sometimes the spouse is the last to know."

"If you believe that," the man with the gruff voice said, "then you're even dumber than that greasy-haired kid on *Jersey Shore!*"

A blast of laughter, and then he resumed speaking. "Claudia Prescott is a scheming liar just like her husband, and I hope they both get a lengthy prison sentence. I say lock 'em up and throw away the key!"

Claudia's eyes burned and her nose itched. She coughed, ran a hand over her chest to alleviate the burning. It felt like someone had poured Russian vodka down her throat, and the more she swallowed the stronger it burned. Their words cut with the precision of a blade, sliced so deep she'd never be whole again. Stealing went against everything she'd been taught, and although Claudia didn't know the two men, for some crazy reason she cared what they thought.

"The Prescotts used investors' money to fund their extravagant lifestyle. They have luxury cars, residential properties and even a three-hundred-foot yacht. Can you believe that? Their victims are penniless, left with nothing but crippling debt, and they're living the good life."

Claudia dug her fingernails into her armrest. She didn't dare turn around, didn't dare open her mouth to defend herself. Let them talk. They didn't know about her charity work, or the community projects she'd donated her time to. She was innocent, and that was all that mattered. *Then why do I feel like curling into a ball and sobbing into my travel pillow?*

Overcome by a strong, distinct scent, Claudia shot up straight in her chair. Terror struck, causing fear to ricochet off the walls of her chest. It couldn't be... He couldn't be here in the first-class lounge, could he? Circa 1840 wasn't just any cologne. The scarcity of the ingredients and the six-month fermentation process made it the most unique fragrance in the world. And, at a thousand dollars a bottle, the most expensive. Her ex-husband wore it because he liked flaunting his wealth. And obviously someone else in the first-class lounge did, too.

"How are you today?"

Claudia blinked and turned toward the man with the rich, deep voice. His tone was soft, as smooth as honey. She narrowed her eyes and hit him with a leave-me-the-hell-alone look. He didn't budge. Instead of making himself scarce, he extended his hand, offering a white cup brimming with whipped cream.

"You look like you could use a warm drink. How about a cup of hot chocolate?"

"No, thanks."

"Please, take it. I insist."

Stepping forward, he rested the drink on the table beside her. His scent drifted over her, hitting her square in the nose. Her stomach heaved, pitched from left to right, coiled in a knot so tight she couldn't swallow.

"I'm Santiago."

"Good for you."

"I brought lunch." He held up a clear plastic bag. "I hope soup, sandwiches and chocolate brownies are okay."

"Do I know you?"

"Not yet. I've been here for hours, and if I keep playing solitaire on my iPhone I'll go crazy," he confessed, sporting a grin that revealed straight, white teeth. "To pass the time I thought we could talk."

Claudia rolled her eyes. What was the matter with these guys? This was the fifth one to hit on her since she'd arrived at the lounge. Only this man in the tan sports coat, white button-down shirt and dark slacks was dreamy. Gorgeous, actually. A Hollywood casting director's dream client. He had a full head of short, wavy black hair, grayish-brown eyes that twinkled with mirth and a smile as blinding as a solar eclipse. Over six feet of lean, muscular man and not a gold tooth in sight. Certainly a step up from the gangster who'd swaggered over earlier. "Look, I'm sure you're a nice guy, but I'm just not interested. I don't want to get to know you better or hook up the next time I'm in town, either. I just want to be left alone. Got it?"

"We'll have lunch together, and then I'll be on my way."

"I'm not hungry." As the lie fell off her lips, her stomach erupted in protest, howling louder than a band of coyotes.

If she didn't eat soon, lounge security would be peeling her up off the floor, and the last thing Claudia wanted was more public humiliation. She was starving, but she didn't want to break bread with this immaculately groomed pretty boy with polished shoes. "I don't have much of an appetite."

Another howl, but this one was accompanied by a sharp hunger pang.

"You're not going to let a nice guy like me eat all alone, are you?"

Coughing to disguise the rumblings in her belly, she opened her wallet and fished out a twenty-dollar bill. "Fine, but I insist on paying you for the food. Will this cover it?"

"Miss, please put away your money. Buying you lunch is my pleasure."

Before Claudia knew what was happening, he sat down and rested the plastic bag on the table between them. A savory aroma filled the air. Growing hungrier with each passing second, she licked the dryness from her lips and accepted the container he graciously offered.

"When I flew in this morning the skies were clear and blue, but now the rain is giving the city a beating," he said, settling comfortably in the chair beside her. "I hope the weather advisory lifts soon. This is a nice lounge, but I don't want to sleep here!"

He chuckled, but Claudia didn't join in his laughter. She concentrated on eating her minestrone soup. Spooning baby carrots into her mouth, she pretended not to notice him watching her. His eyes were laser beams, piercing her flesh and heightening her fear. Something about him was gnawing at her. It was…his cologne. "Are you wearing Circa 1840?"

His eyebrows fused together. "Wow, you really know your colognes."

"My ex wore it for years. It's a nice fragrance, but I think it's way too expensive."

"Do you think there's something wrong with people enjoying the fruits of their wealth?"

"Not if it's earned by honest means, but most millionaires make it rich by exploiting others." Claudia paused, thought a moment and said, "The cost of one bottle could feed a hundred people in my city Thanksgiving dinner, and I think providing the basic necessities of life is far more important than smelling good."

He didn't respond, just nodded and leaned back in his seat.

"I'm sorry," she said, with a small shrug of her shoulders. "I didn't mean to lay a guilt trip on you. What you choose to do with your money is none of my business."

"No harm done. We're just talking, right?"

Still hungry, she reached into the bag and unwrapped one of the sandwiches. She took a bite and sighed in contentment. Claudia didn't bother to hide her pleasure. Loaded with vegetables and barbeque sauce, the sandwich was delicious and tasted even better than it looked.

"Now that we're friends, I think it's only fair that you tell me your name."

To buy herself some time, she picked up the hot chocolate and tasted it. *This Santiago guy isn't half bad,* she thought, as the hot, creamy liquid warmed her body. He was generous, outgoing and seriously cute. Back in the day Claudia would have given him her number, but now she knew better. Knew that no matter how nice a guy seemed he was still just a man. Someone capable of breaking her heart, and killing her hopes and dreams.

"I'm still waiting for that name…"

"It's Claudia."

"A lovely name for a lovely lady." A smile pinched his cheeks, and a set of dimples emerged. "What part of Mexico are you going to?"

"What makes you think I'm going to Mexico?"

He pointed at her purse, and Claudia followed the route of

his gaze. The travel book she'd purchased at the terminal's bookstore was peeking out from behind her makeup case.

"I was born and raised there, so if you have any questions just ask."

Claudia cleaned her mouth with a napkin. She wanted to tell him to get lost, wanted to send him on his way, but she didn't. How could she when he'd brought her such a tasty lunch? They were stuck in the airport, marooned until the storm passed, so why not use the time chatting with this sexy Latino guy about Cabo San Lucas?

Chapter 3

Santiago cursed under his breath.

The men sitting behind him were talking so loud he couldn't hear what Claudia was saying. He thought of telling Beavis and Butthead to shut up, but he didn't want her to think he was rude. Keeping his frustration in check was harder than riding a mechanical bull on quicksand, and when the pair erupted in boisterous laughter, drowning out Claudia's melodious voice, he almost snatched them both up by the collar. How was he supposed to get to know the Southern beauty with these two clowns guffawing every five seconds?

Glad she was finally starting to relax, he carefully studied her appearance. The short, bouncy hair, that shapely body clad in pink-trimmed workout gear. Claudia was the kind of woman his friend Chaz Romero would call a dime piece. Claudia wasn't a nine or a ten, she was a twenty. He'd dated some in his life, and had even been in love a time or two, but he'd never been this drawn to a female, never been so enamored with anyone. "Does everything taste okay?" Santiago saw the deep frown on her face, and worried he'd bought the wrong thing. "I can run and grab you something else if you'd like."

"This sandwich is delicious, but I can't believe it cost fifteen dollars," she said, staring at the red price sticker on the wrapper. "That's really expensive for a chicken-turkey club."

She spoke so softly, so quietly, it was impossible to hear her over the noise. Santiago leaned forward in his chair. Her accent was subtle, distinctly Southern, and rich with femininity.

"If my sister hadn't given me her Priority Pass I wouldn't have even known this lounge existed. I can't believe the daily rate is a hundred dollars. That's highway robbery!"

"You're right, but it's great having somewhere quiet to go to when the airport's packed and you have an extended layover," he said, inclining his head toward her. "And they make the best steak subs here. I've already had three!"

His iPhone rang. Offering an apologetic smile, he slipped a hand into his shirt pocket and hit the End button. He'd bet it was the same woman who'd called an hour ago. The stick-thin cosmetics heiress his mother was trying to set him up with. No way, no thanks. If he ever decided to settle down he'd do the choosing. Not his matchmaking mom.

"Aren't you going to answer your phone?"

"They'll call back."

"Won't your wife worry if you don't pick up?"

Santiago displayed his left hand. "I've happily single."

"Sure you are." Her laugh carried a hard, bitter edge. "That's what they all say."

"Are you meeting up with someone in Mexico?" He found her eyes, saw how the edges darkened, and tried to reach her with his smile. "Or are you traveling solo?"

"You ask a lot of questions."

He shrugged. "I'm just curious."

"*Curious* is a polite word for 'nosy.'"

Santiago chuckled. *So much for her being shy. She's as feisty as a caged lioness!* "My mother is a very social person, and I guess I inherited that trait from her." At the thought of his mother a grin pinched his lips. She was dying for him to get married, anxious to begin spoiling her first grandchild, but he wasn't in the market for a bride and that wasn't going to change any time soon. "Excuse me for being so forward. I mean no harm."

"I don't know anyone there. I'm on my own."

He waited, expected her to say more, but she didn't. "You're going to love Cancun," he began, fishing for information. "There's tons to see and do, and they have some great nightclubs."

"I'm not going to Cancun. I'm—" She started and stopped twice, then released a long, deep sigh. It was if breathing was too much for her, a boring, arduous task that she'd rather not do. Finally, after what seemed like an hour, she said, "I'm going to Cabo San Lucas."

His ears perked up. "What a coincidence. So am I."

Claudia said nothing, just put a hand to her hair and ran her fingers through her bangs.

"If we ever leave this airport and make it down there I'd love to see you again. Maybe we could go out for coffee." Santiago smiled. "Or would you prefer hot chocolate?"

"I won't have time."

Reaching into his attaché case, he retrieved one of his business cards and offered it to her. "If you change your mind or need someone to show you around, give me a call."

Claudia stared at the card as if it was covered in germs. "My week is pretty full."

"I understand."

When she turned away, he eased forward in his chair and dropped it into her purse.

"Do you know much about the resorts in the Tourist Corridor?" she asked, her voice low and filled with hesitation.

"I don't care about the bars or restaurants in the area. I just want to be somewhere safe. And quiet."

A grin claimed his lips. She was staying in the heart of the city? What a stroke of good fortune! He thought of asking the name of her hotel, but didn't want to be accused of being nosy again. "You'll be perfectly safe in and around the peninsula. Because of the surge in celebrity tourists over the last few years, the police have upped their presence in the area."

"Can't afford to let anything happen to the rich and famous, huh?"

Santiago frowned. There was that edge in her voice again. *I wonder what that's all about?* "Tourism is big business in Mexico, and in these hard economic times, every dollar spent in the country counts." He studied her for a moment, trying to make all the pieces of the puzzle fit. "I'm surprised you're not interested in checking out some of the clubs."

A scowl pinched her lips. "Why? Do I look like the kind of woman who enjoys dancing on tables and stumbling around drunk?"

"No, but you look like a dancer, and all of the ones I know love a good party."

"I haven't danced in years. *And,*" she stressed, "pirouettes aren't exactly a crowd-pleaser." Claudia crossed her legs, shifted around in her seat as if she was sitting on a cold, hard cinder block rather than on a plush chair. "Did you study dance, too?"

Santiago cracked up, but when he thought about all those sweltering afternoons he'd spent in that airless dance studio, his laughter fizzled. He'd never see Marisol dance again, never hear the excitement in her voice when she spoke about her passion for the arts. She was gone, forever, and he was to blame. Memories of that fateful night weighed on his chest like a slab of steel, making every breath a fight, a struggle.

"Karate was more my speed, but my younger sister studied ballet for years." He tasted sadness in his mouth, and swallowed hard to wash it away. "Did you ever consider making a career out of it or auditioning for Julliard?"

Her eyebrows rose. "You're very knowledgeable about ballet."

"And you're skilled at evading questions."

A smile caressed her lips, but it was gone so fast Santiago was sure he'd imagined it. He watched her pick up her cup of hot chocolate. Why was she shaking? Was she cold, scared or both? "It might help to talk about it," he said quietly.

Hot chocolate sloshed onto the table when Claudia slapped down her cup and surged to her feet. She was breathing hard, fast, as if she'd just finished sprinting up a flight of stairs.

"Where are you going?"

Claudia tossed her things into her travel bag and yanked violently on the zipper.

"They haven't made any boarding announcements yet." Angry at himself for scaring her off, he rose from his seat and offered a sincere, heartfelt apology. "I didn't mean to upset you, Claudia. Please stay and finish your food."

"I'm done, now if you'll excuse me—"

Santiago did the unthinkable. He rested a hand on her arm and gave a light squeeze. Her flesh was warm, supple, and her fragrance wrapped itself around him like a wisteria vine.

Time crawled to a stop.

Their gazes locked, and for a half second Santiago forgot where he was. Her eyes drew him in, seduced him as surely as Eve and that shiny red apple. He could almost see the energy pulsing between them, could almost smell the perfume of her desire. It was so crippling he felt like he'd been struck by lightning. Lust barreled through him, rooted his hands to her arms and his feet to the ground. Unable to move, he waited for the temporary paralysis to lift, waited impatiently for his thoughts to clear.

Thunder clapped, shaking Santiago out of his dreamlike state.

"I—I have to go."

With a heaviness in his heart, he stepped aside to let her pass, but not before saying, "God is bigger than your problems."

She hesitated a fraction, as if considering his words.

"He'll give you the strength you need to overcome—"

A laugh fell out of her lips. "Yeah, sure, whatever you say." Wearing a scowl that could scare the devil, she grabbed her bag and fled the lounge as if it was engulfed in ten-foot flames.

His eyes followed her every move. Through the restaurant, past the spa and back out into Terminal One. Claudia was as mysterious as the pathway of the wind, and the polar opposite of the women his mother forced on him, but he found her candor refreshing. And her beauty only enhanced her appeal. Santiago loved his mom, but he was sick of going out on dates with fake, pretentious women who cared only about caviar, champagne and shopping sprees in Milan. He was taken by this soft-spoken Southern beauty. She was real, honest, interested in the well-being of her fellow man. He had to see her again.

Santiago returned to his seat. There were a lot of perks to being a Medina, and he planned to use every connection he had to track her down. And hopefully the next time he saw Claudia she wouldn't run from their undeniable connection.

"Ma'am, I'm going to have to ask you to put away your cell phone."

Claudia kept her eyes glued to the screen. She read her sister's text message again, unsure what to make of it.

The suite isn't ready yet but hang tight.

What was that supposed to mean? If there was an issue with the room, she wanted to hear about it. Now. Before the plane took off. Lynchburg was a far cry from staying at a luxury resort in Cabo San Lucas, but it was better than nothing.

"Ma'am, did you hear me?"

Claudia held up a finger. "I'll just be a minute. I need to call my sister."

"I'm not going to ask you again."

Stunned by the flight attendant's rudeness, she cranked her head toward her, wondering how a woman with dimples could be so evil. "It's an emergency."

Glaring at her as if she'd been caught coloring on the cabin walls with permanent marker, the bony redhead stuck a hand to her size zero waist and tapped her high heel impatiently on the floor. "This is nonnegotiable. Everyone has to adhere to the safety policies in place, including you."

What is this? "Dump on Claudia" Day? She wanted to cry—to release all the pent-up emotion she'd been holding inside—but after spending six miserable hours at the Dulles International Airport she didn't have the strength crying required.

Summoning a smile, she eased forward in her seat and struck down all thoughts of yanking the attendant's frizzy hair. "I've just discovered that—"

"If you don't put your cell phone away right this minute I'm going to call airport security and have you escorted off this flight." She talked with her hands, flapping them around like an inebriated traffic cop. "Now, what's it going to be?"

Realizing she was fighting a losing battle, Claudia closed her phone and stuffed it into her pocket. "I don't understand what the problem is. Passengers are still boarding the plane and the pilot announced that takeoff wouldn't be for several more minutes."

"New rules. Take it up with the airline."

Claudia wanted to smack the smirk off the stewardess's face, but instead she grabbed the trashy tabloid magazine from the pocket in front of her. *Things could be worse,* she decided, scanning the salacious headlines. *At least I'm not stuck in Richmond.*

A leggy flight attendant sidled up to Ms. Bossy Pants.

"I got one more in first class," she whispered, fanning her face with her hands. "And he's so friggin' sexy I could lick him all over!"

Seated behind the curtain that separated the two cabins, Claudia had a clear view into first class and spotted the new arrival the moment he stepped onto the plane. It was…Santiago. The guy who'd bought her lunch. Claudia prayed she'd go unnoticed in her cheap economy-class seat. No such luck. His gaze zeroed in on her, and a searing, blistering heat spread from her ears to her toes. *He sure is easy on the eyes,* she thought, feeling a rush of desire. He had the classic facial features of a model, a cluster of jet-black curls, and a chest her hands were desperate to kiss and caress. *Great, now I sound like that horny flight attendant.*

Santiago flashed a thousand-watt smile, one intended to make her drool. And she did. All over her scoop-neck shirt. He waved as if they were dear old friends, and like a fool, she waved, too. Claudia pushed a hand through her hair and swept her bangs up off her face. She was attracted to him, but that didn't mean she was interested in making a love connection. Chemistry was overrated. So was confidence, charisma and all of the other qualities he possessed. Forget sexual attraction, fiery French kisses and earth-shattering sex. That stuff was for Hollywood. In the real world, love didn't last and desire waned faster than quick-drying paint.

Sliding the magazine down past her nose, she combed her eyes over his lean frame. Claudia felt an instant connection to him, something she'd never experienced, and the more she stared at him, the higher her temperature rose. He had a handsome face, a perfect body and a voice dripping with sensuality. Too bad she wasn't impressed. She'd met dozens of men like him before and had been disappointed by each and every one. From now on she was only dating regular guys, blue-collar workers who understood the value of a dollar earned and spent responsibly. And she was staying the hell away from that Holy Bible thumper sitting in first class. What was it he'd said? Some mumbo jumbo about God being there in times of need. *I bet he believes in the tooth fairy, too!* she thought, smirking. Her life had been full of setbacks, one after another, and she'd experienced heartbreak at every turn. No, God definitely didn't care about her. If he did, he wouldn't allow bad things to keep happening to her.

Her gaze slid from Santiago to Ms. Bossy Pants, and when the redhead disappeared into the gallery, Claudia sprung into action. Tossing the magazine aside, she opened her cell phone, punched in her sister's number, and waited impatiently for the call to connect. "Pick up, pick up," she chanted, crouching down in her seat. "Come on, dammit. Pick up."

"Hello?"

Claudia exhaled. "Max, it's me. What's wrong with the suite?"

"Hey, girl. What's up? Are you still stuck in Washington?"

"I don't have time to chitchat. Tell me what's going on."

"One of Royce's old college buddies is staying in the suite."

Her spirits plummeted, fell so fast she felt dizzy. "Why didn't you check with Royce before you offered it to me?"

"It's not my fault," Maxine argued. "He never said a word to me about Dimitri being there until I mentioned that you were headed to Cabo."

"When's this guy leaving?"

"In a couple days. He'll probably be gone before you get there, but I wanted to give you a heads-up just in case." Her voice brightened. "Everything'll be fine. Don't sweat it."

"That's easy for you to say. You're not the one who could end up out on the street."

"And neither will you. The suite has two master bedrooms,

an enormous living room and more than enough space for the both of you."

Shaking her head, Claudia decided her sister was even crazier than she thought. "Forget it, Max. I'm not going to stay in the suite with a perfect stranger."

"He doesn't have to be..." Max giggled. "Dimitri's tall, supercute, and built like a Ram truck. What more could you want in a sex buddy?"

"I'm not interested."

"Milk's not the *only* thing that does a body good. Hot sex does wonders, too!"

"Now I know how you managed to get knocked up on your second date."

"Don't hate, congratulate!" Her voice turned serious. "There have been some new developments in William's case that I thought you should know about. He was deemed a flight risk by the judge this afternoon in court, and was denied bail."

"Good. I hope he never gets out."

"The feds confiscated his computers, but they haven't uncovered anything incriminating yet."

Hearing a noise at the rear of the plane, Claudia twisted around in her seat. Fear surged through her, causing her heartbeat to thunder in her ears. The flight attendant from hell was stomping toward her, gaining on her with each step. "I have to go! She's coming!"

"Who—"

Click.

Claudia tossed her cell phone into her purse, snatched the blanket off the vacant seat beside her, and dragged it up to her chin. Scared the flight attendant would make good on her earlier threat, she closed her eyes and started to snore.

The lights dimmed and a hush fell over the cabin.

"Excuse me, miss. Can you hold this open for me?"

Opening one eye, Claudia watched as Santiago slid in front of Ms. Bossy Pants. His muscles flexed, drew taut against the

light fabric of his shirt as he hoisted his travel bag into the
overhead bin. He glanced over his shoulder, and for a long,
heart-pounding moment Claudia couldn't breathe. Every time
he looked at her she experienced respiratory failure. What
was up with that? To keep from slobbering all over herself
like one of her sister's chocolate Labs, she turned her face
toward the tiny cabin window.

Thick, somber clouds blackened the sky, and as the plane
inched down the runway, torrential rains beat violently
against the windows. *The last time I was in a storm this bad
was that night I was rushed to the hospital.* Being strapped
down on that cold, hard gurney had made her feel helpless,
powerless. *Just like now.*

Claudia crossed her legs at her ankles. For now, the mess in
Richmond was behind her. She was safe, free to do whatever
she wanted without public scrutiny. The realization should
have calmed her, should have bolstered her spirits, but as
her eyes grew heavy with sleep another terrifying thought
gripped her. *What if those reporters camped out on my lawn
discover the truth about my past?*

Chapter 4

This is *paradise,* Claudia decided, stepping out of the green Volkswagen taxi and drinking in the lush scenery of the Sea of Cortez Resort. Tranquility showered over her, filled her with such peace that the tension radiating through her body began to subside. *If everything I read in that travel book is true I may never leave!*

Nestled on golden sands that stretched for miles, the five-building structure drenched in white and gold was a lavish display of luxury and wealth. Designed to reflect the rich heritage of the Mexican culture, the Sea of Cortez Resort had been constructed with such historic flair, it stood out from the dozens of other hotels along the Tourist Corridor.

Two uniformed men with bodies like Chippendale dancers appeared at her side. One placed a cocktail glass in her hand while the other scooped up her lone travel bag. *"Deje todo para trás y escape al paraíso!"*

Claudia didn't know what they said, but did it matter when they sounded dreamy and smelled like tropical fruit? Deciding it didn't, she hitched herself to her attractive escorts. Wishing she'd paid more attention during her high school Spanish classes, she strung together the few sentences she knew and hoped for the best. *"Gracias tanto. Usted es el más amable."*

"It is my pleasure to serve you, señorita. Now leave everything behind and escape to paradise," one of the men said in a deep, silky baritone. "Your adventure awaits!"

That's music to my ears, she thought, discreetly cleaning the dots of perspiration along her hairline. Carrying the scent of the water lilies floating in the pond, the evening wind blew hot and fast against her sweaty skin. To quench her thirst, Claudia sipped from the pink, candy-flavored straw. The lemon tickled her taste buds, and the combination of tequila and grenadine packed a powerful punch. Navigating her way through Cabo's bustling airport had been an exercise in stamina and patience, and after a forty-minute wait for a taxi an ice-cold cocktail was just what the doctor ordered.

"¿Puedo despertar su interés en otro Amanecer de Cortez?"

Claudia blinked, and when her escort traded her empty glass for a new one, she smiled sheepishly. Then gulped it down in ten seconds flat. Knocking back cocktails wasn't the answers to her problems, but they sure did taste good!

Lit by the warm glow of tiki torches, the cobbled pathway flowed through wide arches and spilled on to manicured lawns rimmed with leafy bushes. Claudia felt like she was walking through the pearly gates. Palm trees waved their arms in greeting, sunshine rained down from the sky and the scent rising from the garden was more intoxicating than the cocktails she'd downed.

The glass doors slid open, revealing an atrium drenched in bright, vibrant colors. High ceilings, topped with mosaic tiles, filtered in natural sunlight and created the sensation of still being outdoors. Oozing with charm, the main floor lobby featured bronze chandeliers dripping with crystals, oil paintings on crimson walls, and velvet couches that looked cozy enough to sleep on. Or cuddle on. And couples were doing just that. It was almost nine o'clock in the evening, but the resort was teeming with life and activity. Everywhere Claudia turned guests were laughing, chatting and living it up.

Grateful to her escorts, she generously tipped them and joined the line in front of the reception desk. While Claudia waited, she retrieved her wallet and selected two pieces of ID. Traveling had exhausted her, and she was anxious to see the oceanfront suite Maxine had bragged about. She only hoped it was available. If not, she'd just stay in another room because there was no way she was shacking up with Mr. Ram Truck.

"Buenas noches, señorita. Bienvenido a la Estación de Mar de Cortez. ¿Cómo le puedo ayudar?"

Claudia offered a weak smile. She hoped the concierge spoke English, because the little Spanish she knew wasn't enough to carry her through check-in. Before she could speak, he asked for her last name. Relieved that she wouldn't have to break out her travel book, she inquired about Suite 97. "Is it available?"

"Yes, Ms. Jefferies, it is."

Claudia wanted to jump for joy, but smiled instead.

"Is this your first time in Cabo San Lucas?" he asked, punching the necessary information into the computer. "Or are you a regular?"

"I was in Mexico many years ago, but I've never been to Cabo before."

He held up her passport, intently studied her picture. "How long will you be staying with us, Ms. Jeffries?"

"I'm not sure," she told him. "Probably a month."

"That's wonderful! Four weeks is more than enough time to see Cabo and the surrounding cities as well. Might I make a few recommendations of things to do?"

Claudia knew he was just doing his job—making conversation to speed along the process—but after a day filled with delays and disappointments she didn't have energy for small talk. "No thanks. It's been a long day and I'm really looking forward to relaxing in my suite."

"I understand, Ms. Jeffries. All I need is a credit card to cover the incidentals, and then you can be on your way."

Nodding, she unzipped her wallet and handed over her Platinum MasterCard.

"For an additional fee you can add a Luxury Services package to your stay. It features twenty-four-hour housekeeping, private butler service and unlimited access to our world-class spa for the low, low price of only five hundred dollars."

Claudia's mouth hit the limestone counter. Did she look like a sucker? Instead of laughing in the concierge's face, she said, "I think I'll pass."

"Very well. You can always add the service later if you change your mind." The computer beeped, and the smile slid off his face. "I'm sorry, Ms. Jeffries, but there seems to be a problem. Your credit card has been declined."

"What?" Shame burned Claudia's cheeks, made her body so hot she could start a forest fire. "That's impossible. I'm nowhere near the limit."

"Have you made any large purchases in the last few hours? Sometimes that may cause—"

"There must be a problem with your system. Swipe it again."

He did, and this time the computer beeped twice. "I'm sorry. It still won't go through."

Hoping no one had witnessed her humiliation, Claudia peeked over her shoulder. Three suit-clad men holding brief-cases stood behind her, dead quiet. They were listening in and were every bit as annoying as those pesky reporters who'd made themselves at home on her front lawn.

Hanging her head, she shielded her face with her hands.

What if one of them recognized her and alerted the press? She could see the headlines now:

Claudia Jeffries-Prescott spotted in Cabo San Lucas!
Ex-wife of disgraced CEO can't pay bills!
Investors forced to eat in soup kitchens while Prescotts party at world-class resort!

"Do you have another credit card I can charge?"

Claudia dodged the question. "I don't understand what's going on. I've been using this credit card all day," she confessed, pushing out a breath of frustration. "I'll have to call MasterCard and have them straighten this mess out."

He gestured to the end of the counter. "Please, use our house phone."

"Now?" Claudia checked her watch. Nine thirty-seven. No way she was calling MasterCard at this time of night. Forget that. She'd sooner sleep in the lobby than subject herself to an hour-long wait. "I don't plan to order room service or eat from the mini bar, so having my credit card on file is not necessary."

The concierge reared back like he'd been burned with scalding water. Claudia read his facial expression, saw the veins stretched tight in his neck and the lines of doubt etched in his forehead. He didn't trust her any more than those detectives did back in Richmond.

"I simply cannot check you in without a valid credit card, Ms. Jeffries." He must have heard the harshness in his tone, because he softened his voice. "We're not supposed to take cash to cover the cost of the incidentals, but I'm willing to do it to help you out. There's an ATM machine to the right of the guest services booth and…"

Claudia strangled a groan. Even if she had the energy to walk back through the lobby—which she didn't—thanks to the SEC she didn't have access to her bank accounts. And her emergency fund account, which she'd wisely registered in Aunt Hattie's name years earlier, was accessible only through commercial banking. "Can we straighten this out in the morning? I've been traveling for the last eight hours, and I'm exhausted."

A voluptuous brunette, who looked like she'd been stuffed into her tangerine-colored uniform, appeared beside the concierge. "Is there a problem, Luis?"

He spoke quietly, in rapid-fire Spanish.

A minute passed. Then two. Were they still talking about her credit card problems or their plans for the weekend? Claudia wished she spoke Spanish, or knew someone who could help her out of this mess. *I should have taken that Santiago guy's business card,* she thought, mentally berating herself for insulting him and fleeing the airport lounge without his number. It wasn't every day that a perfect stranger bought her lunch, and the Mexican native was sincere and charming. He seemed like the kind of man who made things happen and got things done.

"Registering guests without proper documentation is against company policy," the woman explained in precise English. "And doing so could result in disciplinary action for the both of us."

"I understand that, and once I straighten everything out with the credit card company tomorrow I'll pass that information on to you."

"I'll go speak with my supervisor and see if there's something we can do."

Claudia read the woman's name tag. "Thank you, Rosario. I greatly appreciate it."

"I'll be a few minutes. Make yourself comfortable in the reception area and I'll come get you when I'm done."

In spite of her outward show of calm, Claudia was nervous and scared. Fighting against feelings of despair, she picked up her bag and carried herself over to the lounge. A stiff drink would come in handy right now, she thought, wishing the tray-carrying bellhop was still around. What more could go wrong today? Six months ago, she'd been paid handsomely to plan a magical destination wedding for colleagues turned soul mates, Niveah Evans and Damien Hunter, and now she had more money woes than the late King of Pop.

Claudia took a moment to collect herself. Going to another resort tonight was out of the question, so she'd just have to convince the resort manager to let her stay. What was it Maxine had said? *Smile, giggle and flash a bit of cleavage if you have to!* Claudia hated playing the beauty card, especially because she always felt as inept as the forty-third president addressing the Senate, but if flirting would get her out of the lobby and into that luxury suite she'd channel her inner sex goddess and charm the man's socks off.

Santiago poked his head into the staff lounge, and when he saw his mother lift the sofa love seat and vacuum underneath it, a frown creased his lips. Curiosity drew Santiago inside the room. Tilting his head to the side, he pensively stroked the length of his jaw. His mother's energy level wasn't the only thing that shocked him. Her midsection was flat, and she had arms that would make Wonder Woman jealous.

Santiago watched in stunned disbelief as his mom made quick work of cleaning the lounge. Something smelled fishy, and the odor wasn't coming from the aquarium.

"You're here!" Ana Medina switched off the vacuum. Dropping the handle, she shot across the room and threw her arms around her son. "Welcome home, Tiago!"

Santiago chuckled and returned her hug. "Thanks, Mom. It's good to see you."

"When did you get in?"

"About an hour ago. I dropped my bags off in the office, then came looking for you. Why are you cleaning?"

"We're short-staffed today, and I couldn't stand to see this room dirty any longer. Just because we own the resort doesn't mean I can't do our part to help out."

"And you wonder where I get my tireless work ethic from," he teased, winking at her.

"Enough about work. Stand still and let me get a good look at you." Slipping off her eyeglasses, she studied him for a long, hard minute. "You get more handsome each year. That's hard to believe considering you live in such a wickedly cold place. And a violent one, too."

Santiago hid a smile. "Can I at least have something to eat before you start in on me?"

"I have a pot of salsa simmering at home as we speak," she explained, her voice filled with cheer. "I'm making all your favorites tonight. Pea soup, Spanish rice, and beef enchiladas."

"You're supposed to be taking it easy." He watched her, saw how she dodged his gaze and shifted her feet. "Has the hospital finally confirmed the date and time for your surgery?"

Ana clutched his hands. "Great news, Tiago! The surgery's been cancelled. Most of my symptoms have disappeared and the few that remain are quite minor."

"Is that so?"

"I decided to try some of the things my doctor suggested, and I've been getting stronger each day. I take ginseng three times a day, quit drinking alcohol and started cooking healthier, low-calorie meals, too."

"Exactly how much weight have you lost?"

She shrugged and stared down at the sleek tiled floor. "Just a little."

"How much?" he pressed, crossing his arms. "Ten? Fifteen? Twenty pounds?"

"Twenty-seven, give or take."

Santiago clamped his lips together to trap a curse inside. "You were never scheduled to have abdominal surgery, were you? That was just a ploy to get me down here, wasn't it?"

"Of course not!" The words shot out of her mouth with

more force than a bullet from a gun. Anger crimped her features, but her tone was soft. "I would never lie about something as serious as that. I was scared about going under the knife, so I changed my entire lifestyle."

"It's hard to believe you lost almost thirty pounds by just altering your diet."

"Tiago, don't be ridiculous! The weight didn't just vanish. I've been working my tush off!" Her smile was proud. "I've been swimming and hiking and playing a little squash."

"You're exercising?" Santiago dropped his hands on his waist like an exasperated father about to scold his child. "Who are you? And what have you done with my mother?"

Laughter bubbled out from her lips. "Now that your father's overseeing the construction of the new golf resort in Acapulco, I have more time to try new things."

"I'm glad you're feeling better, Mom. I just wish you would've told me your surgery was cancelled sooner."

"I only found out yesterday," she said, with a shrug of her shoulders.

Santiago didn't believe her, but he wasn't stupid enough to call his mother a liar.

"I'm glad you're here, Tiago. I was convinced you'd forgotten all about me."

He tossed his head back and had a good laugh. "Right, like you'd ever let *that* happen."

"Your father and I have missed you dearly, son."

Deep down, Santiago knew only half of what his mother said was true, but he inquired about his dad anyway. "How's he doing?" To expunge the bitter taste in his mouth, he swallowed hard. "Is he still dead set against attending counseling with you?"

"Yes, he said hearing other people's stories of loss only compounds his grief."

"Figures. Dad's never been one to share his feelings."

"That's why I need you around, Tiago. You're the only one

who understands what I'm going through, and the only person I can talk to when I'm feeling down."

"Is he still drinking?"

Ana shook her head, diverted her gaze. "He hardly touches the stuff anymore. Honestly, I can't remember the last time he had a drink."

Sure you don't. He saw the truth in her eyes, saw the flicker of hurt that flashed across her face. His dad was still a raging alcoholic, and knowing that he was the cause of his father's downward spiral made Santiago feel sick with guilt.

"When are you going to move home and help me run the resort?"

"When you stop throwing your friends' daughters at me."

Mrs. Medina slipped an arm around her son's waist. "Find yourself a nice girl from a nice Mexican family and I will!"

Santiago chuckled when his mom wagged her finger at him. Then, she sighed dramatically and launched into her famous I-want-grandchildren-before-I-die speech. The one she repeated faithfully every week. To get his mother off his back, he considered telling her about Claudia, but thought better of it. Besides, what would he say? *Hey, Mom, I met a stunningly beautiful woman at the airport who I felt an instant connection to, but I stupidly chased her off.*

While his mother talked, he replayed every minute of his conversation with Claudia in his mind. He wondered where she was and what she was doing. Was she reclining by the pool at her hotel? Or fighting off the men at the bar while she sipped her drink? No doubt about that. He'd seen firsthand the kind of attention she drew, saw how grown men tripped and stumbled over themselves in her presence. Not that he blamed them. Claudia had it all—flawless skin that had a soft, natural glow, eyes that penetrated, and an endearing shyness that made him want to protect her, hold her, take her in his arms and make everything wrong in her life better.

"I'm just not ready to take that step," he admitted, hoping

to put an end to her complaints once and for all. "I'll get married and have kids in God's time and not a moment sooner."

His mother sniffed, rubbed her fingertips slowly under her eyes.

"I'm sorry, Mom. I didn't mean to upset you."

"You didn't. It's just, now that your sister's gone, you're all I have left. And it kills me only seeing you once or twice a year." Wearing a sad smile, she patted his cheeks as if he was a little boy rather than a grown man. "It would mean the world to me if you returned home."

Hearing the anguish in his mother's voice made Santiago feel lower than the gecko slithering outside the window. He cleared his throat, but the burning in his chest only intensified. The stench of his guilt was stifling, thicker than smoke, and suddenly the staff lounge felt smaller than an airplane bathroom.

"I promised your father I wouldn't say anything, but if I have to speak my mind—"

"Ramón, there's a problem out front I need you to take care of." The female clerk standing in the doorway bowed slightly. "I apologize for interrupting, Señora Medina, but I was wondering if you've seen Ramón. I can't find him anywhere."

"Tomorrow's his daughter's Quinceañera, so I let him go early," she explained, waving her inside. "Rosario, there's someone special I'd like you to meet."

Knowing what was coming next, Santiago braced himself for impact. He only prayed his mother wouldn't ask the clerk out on his behalf. The last time she did, he'd been tricked into escorting a chatty fashion designer to a black-tie event.

"This very handsome, *very* single young man is my son, Santiago. He'll be returning to Cabo soon to take over running the resort, and I'm depending on you and the rest of the staff to show him how things are done around here."

Santiago frowned. Moving back to Cabo? To run the family business? No way, no how. There were too many memories, too much pain. And every time he saw the hate in his father's eyes he was reminded of that tragic summer night. It was hard enough waking up each morning as it was; he didn't need a daily reminder of what a screw-up he was, too.

"I'll try my best, Señora Medina."

"Now, what's going on out front? You look upset." Ana stuck a hand on her hip. "It's not that South African diplomat again, is it? That horny old man is testing my patience, and if he propositions another female maid I'm tossing him out on his rear!"

Rosario explained the source of her troubles. "I feel bad for Ms. Jeffries, but I'm apprehensive about granting her request. The last time I allowed a couple to stay in a suite without a valid credit card, they pilfered the mini bar and trashed the room."

"I remember. That's why we revised our check-in policies last year," Ana said with a fervent nod. "How long is she planning to stay?"

"A month."

"I see. All right, let her pay in cash to cover the cost of the incidentals."

"I suggested that," Rosario explained. "She refused."

"If she doesn't have a hundred dollars in her bank account, then how can she afford to stay here for a month?"

"I was wondering the same thing."

"I'll get to the bottom of this." Ana stepped forward, then swiveled around and grabbed Santiago's arm. "On second thought, you go handle it. It's about time you got your feet wet, and what better way to get acquainted with our policies than by manning the front desk?"

"This is not exactly my area of expertise," he pointed out, taking a giant step back. "I'm a business consultant, not a hotel manager. I don't know the first thing about operating a resort."

"Don't worry. Rosario will be right there to help you." Ana

pecked his cheek. "I'm going home to finish dinner, but I'll see you in an hour."

A wave and she was gone, fleeing the lounge at breakneck speed.

Rosario laughed. "Your mom is quite the woman."

"You can say that again."

"Shall we go?"

Santiago nodded and reluctantly followed the brunette down the hall. He'd only arrived an hour ago, but his mother had already duped him twice. *God help me,* he prayed, releasing a tortured sigh, *because at this rate she'll have me married off by the end of the week!*

Chapter 5

"She was just here," Rosario said, gesturing to the red wing-back chair she'd left Ms. Jeffries sitting in. "I don't know where she could have gone."

Santiago didn't know what Ms. Jeffries looked like, but he aided in the search. Walking through the lobby with Rosario fretting at his side, he kept his eyes open for the mystery guest with the bogus credit card. The resort was filled with excitement, and he felt reenergized by the activities around him. Tourists decked out in formal attire snapped pictures in front of the hand-painted mural, businessmen smoking cigars fervently argued politics and an all-female group sipped cocktails at the bar. Their high-pitched laughter mingled with the song the mariachi band was playing and added to the jovial mood on the main floor.

"Don't tell me to calm down! I have every right to be upset. You encouraged me to come down here and now I'm screwed!"

Startled by the harshness of the female's voice, Santiago

cast a glance over his shoulder in search of the bickering couple. There was no guy in sight. Just a woman on her cell phone, crouched down, digging around in an oversize pink travel bag. Santiago's tongue tumbled out of his mouth and hit his chest with the force of a fifty-pound dumbbell.

Claudia was here. At his parents' resort. Her back was to him, but he'd recognize that tight, perfectly shaped tush anywhere. Claudia had a beautiful face, but her backside was twice as nice. The sister had a killer body, the kind of shape that caused whiplash and made grown men slobber all over themselves.

And she did it for him in a major way.

Stopping abruptly, he spun around, and walked back across the lobby toward her. His shoes pounded on the tile floor, competing with the deafening sound of his heartbeat. Santiago wondered if the on-site physician was available, because seeing Claudia left him rattled, woozy, like he'd been struck upside the head with a bag of pesos.

Santiago picked up his pace. He had to get to her before someone else did. A big believer in fate, he knew that running into Claudia again was more than just a coincidence. This was his chance to make a *second* first impression, and he intended to make the most of it.

His senses on high alert, he blocked out the noises crowding the lobby and listened intently to what she was saying into the phone.

"This is what I get for listening to you. I should have never come down here, Max."

Santiago frowned. Who was Max? And just how serious were they? An air of mystery surrounded Claudia, which made her all the more intriguing, but it was going to be impossible to get close to her. She hated men, hated God, and was angry at the world. How could he ever win?

"There she is!" Rosario shrieked, flapping her hands like

a bald eagle taking flight. "She's standing at the north entrance."

A grin crimped Santiago's lips. *Claudia Jeffries.* Now that he had her full name, he could set his plan in motion. One roadblock down, and only two left to go.

"I'm so glad we found her," she admitted, relief washing over her face. "I was worried she'd tricked one of the maids into letting her into that suite. You'd be amazed at how often that happens around here. The Australian national rugby team is in town for a tournament, and just yesterday I caught the captain fooling around with a *pollita* in the Presidential suite. Turns out someone on staff accidentally let them in."

Santiago wore a confused expression. "I'm sorry, Rosario, but what did you say the woman's name was again?"

"Claudia Jeffries."

"What a small world," he said, making his eyes wide. "I know her. Claudia's a business associate of mine, and I can vouch for her. She won't stiff us. She'll make good on her bill."

Rosario didn't argue. "Okay, Mr. Medina, wait right here. I'll go to the front desk and get her a key card for Suite 1164."

"Do me a favor and add the Luxury Services package to her stay."

"It was offered, but she declined."

"Then I'll absorb the cost." Santiago thought back to their conversation in the airport lounge, remembered the sadness in her voice, the deep pain in her eyes and her lifeless movements. Claudia needed someone to look out for her, and he was just the man for the job. "Are there any apartments available in Oasis Row?"

"Last time I checked there were several."

Santiago made an executive decision. One that would take Claudia away from the main building and the crowd. To improve his chances of getting to know her, he had to see her every day. And not just see her, but talk, interact, share. So he told Rosario to book her into one of their private, oceanfront apartments. Now, she was just a stone's throw away from his suite, and he wouldn't have to worry about some ripped rugby player sweeping Claudia off her feet. "Ask Chaz to prepare one of his famous vegetarian meals for her tonight."

"As you wish, sir. I'll go put in the order now."

Sweat snaked down his back. Licking his lips, he discreetly cleaned the perspiration from his palms. This time he was going to be the perfect gentleman. He wouldn't scare her off or come on too strong. He'd listen. And help. That was it. Santiago was curious about the Southern beauty, and he was going to get to learn more about her. Starting now.

Claudia bent down, unzipped her travel bag and searched for the bottle of Tylenol she'd hurled inside it that morning. Her head hurt so bad her eyes were twitching, but she had bigger problems than a raging headache. Where was she going to stay? And what was she going to say to the resort manager? Claudia felt a presence behind her, and knew that it was a guy. No surprise there. Her butt was poking up in the air. That usually brought perverts running.

"Bug off, buddy. I'm not interested."

To project self-assurance, Santiago raised his head and straightened his shoulders. She did a half turn and hit him with such a scathing look. His heart stopped dead in his chest. As they stood there, eyeing each other, he realized two things: Claudia wasn't going to accept his help, and he was in way over his head. He suspected that her brusque exterior was a cover, a mask to shield her from pain, and if he wanted to penetrate her walls he had to be real.

Take baby steps, cautioned his inner voice, *baby steps.* Confidence soared through his veins, renewed his optimism and hope. He'd take things slow, let her be the one to dictate the pace. He desired her but he wasn't going to cross the line. *I'm going to be a gentleman even if it kills me,* he vowed, tearing his hungry gaze away from her long legs. "We meet again."

Claudia's lips parted and a gasp fell out. It was the smokin'-hot guy who'd approached her at the Dulles International Airport. "Did you follow me here?"

"No, I..." Santiago hesitated, paused to organize his scrambled thoughts. Telling her his family owned the Sea of Cortez Resort, and six other luxury hotels across Mexico, wasn't a smart move. She'd think he was lying or, worse, just another cocksure rich guy who liked to brag. No, now was definitely not the time to reveal his true identity. "I work here."

Pain pulsed in her head, but she abandoned her search for the aspirin and rose to her feet. Claudia scrutinized him from top to bottom. He wasn't wearing the ubiquitous tangerine shirt, and he didn't have a name tag pinned to his chest. This Santiago guy had to be putting her on, because in his pin-striped shirt and tan slacks he looked more like a guest than an employee. "You work here? In what capacity?"

"I'm the manager," he said, keeping an eye out for any resort staff. If his mother heard him he could kiss his life back in the States goodbye. She'd scream louder than the Dallas Cowboy cheerleaders and pop open her most expensive bottle of champagne. "The front desk called and said you needed to speak to me."

"Is that all they said?"

He had to tread softly, had to phrase his words carefully, in a way that wouldn't offend her. "I understand that there's a problem with your credit card."

All the blood drained from her body. This had to be one of the most embarrassing moments of her life. It ranked right up there with throwing up on her wedding day. Though she realized now that getting sick had been a sign, something she shouldn't have ignored.

"I'm not broke," she told him. "I'm a very successful event

planner, and I have my own business. I could afford to stay at this resort three times over."

"I believe you, Ms. Jeffries, and no one here is accusing you of deceit. The problem could very well be with our system."

Relief flooded through her, alleviated the throbbing in her temples that was radiating down her neck. Finally, someone on her side! Claudia didn't feel comfortable explaining her situation to him, but she felt compelled to offer an explanation for the mishap at the front desk.

"We've been having trouble processing credit card payments all day. It must be a bad connection," he explained. Santiago gauged her reaction. Her face softened, lost some of the angry lines creasing her forehead, but he knew he hadn't completely won her over. Feeling the tide turn in his favor, he decided to play his hunch. "I apologize for the way the front desk handled your check-in. We are short-staffed today and they've had to work long hours."

Santiago spotted a group of brawny, dark-haired men in cranberry-red jerseys stride off the elevator and waited for them to pass before he resumed speaking. "Until we get this whole mess sorted out, I thought you could stay in one of our oceanfront apartments."

Claudia's spirits sank. She should have known this guy was too good to be true. Weren't they all? Some savior he was. Instead of resolving the issue, he was grinning like a televangelist and trying to pump her for more money. Figured. The hospitality industry didn't care about their guests; all they cared about was their bottom line.

"The only drawback of staying in the apartment is that it's away from the main building and in a private, tree-shielded area."

"That sounds like a plus, not a minus." The thought of being alone, miles away from other guests, appealed to her. Maybe she should swing it. Tomorrow she'd go to the bank and withdraw enough money to cover her stay. The only question was what to do now. "I really need the space to unwind. I love live music, but those mariachi singers are louder than a high school marching band!"

Santiago wanted to laugh but stayed in character. He was the resort manager and had to act like such at all times. No guffawing or flirting allowed. "Most of our guests like to be where the action is, and Oasis Row couldn't be more secluded. I have a suite there, and sometimes I don't see anyone for days."

"How much is the daily rate? The suite I'm staying in belongs to my sister and my brother-in-law, so it wasn't costing me anything."

"And neither will an apartment suite."

"How is that possible?"

Yeah, his conscience jeered, *how is that possible?* The question threw him for a loop, but he recovered quickly. "The resort is below capacity, and at the Sea of Cortez Resort we believe that once you experience one of our premier suites you'll never want to stay anywhere else." He wore an arch grin. "At least that's our hope."

She stayed perfectly still, didn't say a word, didn't even blink. Then, something remarkable happened. The corners of her lips twitched, curled like she was about to smile.

"We offer services that other hotels just can't provide, such as in-suite spa treatments, tai chi lessons in our Zen garden, and twenty-four-hour room service."

To keep from whooping for joy, Claudia bit the inside of her cheek. But when Santiago winked at her, a giggle broke free. She was stoked, high, more excited than a preteen girl meeting her favorite pop star. "Thank you. You have no idea how much this means to me."

"Now, if you'll follow me, I'll take you to your suite," Santiago announced, reaching for her travel bag. "I just need to make a quick stop at the front desk to retrieve your room key."

"I don't need you to take me. Point me in the right direction and I'll find my way."

"It's getting dark, Ms. Jeffries, and I'd hate for you to get lost."

Was he patronizing her? Trying to imply that she was incapable of taking care of herself? Claudia snatched her things out of his hand. "Don't worry. I won't."

Rosario appeared, handed him a key card and hustled back to her post.

"It looks like we're all set." Santiago bowed at the waist and swept his hands gallantly toward her. "Here, at the Sea of Cortez Resort, we believe in offering our guests premier service, so I'd be honored to escort you to your villa, Ms. Jeffries."

"And I told you," she repeated, "that won't be necessary."

"It's a company policy." He lowered his voice, then glanced over his shoulder as if he was about to confess his deepest, darkest secret. "And if the owner finds out I broke the rules she'll have my head!"

To put an end to her protests, and get her far away from the shirtless, blue-eyed Adonis who'd just exited the fitness center, Santiago gestured to the courtyard doors. "Shall we go?"

Claudia gave up the fight. "Okay, fine, you can escort me to my suite. You've been terribly kind, and I'd hate for you to lose your job over something so trivial."

"Me too," Santiago said, with a chuckle. "I need this job!"

Decorative lampposts showered the garden with light. The wood-paneled walkway was bordered by two miniature ponds filled with sea turtles, tropical flowers and rocks. In the distance, Claudia heard music and laughter. Through the space in the trees, she spotted a lighted pool teeming with swimmers and kids playing volleyball at the tip of the beach.

As they strolled past the communal bathhouses, Santiago gave her a detailed briefing on the resort. Ten minutes ago, she'd been so tired she'd almost fallen asleep in the lobby and now she was wide awake, alert, hanging on to every word that came out of the resort manager's sexy mouth. "I can't believe the resort has a library! Is there anything you guys don't have here?"

"We're in the process of building several fantasy suites and a wedding chapel. Destination weddings have become incredibly popular in Cabo, and we'd like to offer the service to our out-of-town guests," he explained, repeating what his mother had told him about the project weeks earlier. "How long have you been a wedding planner?"

"Event planner," she corrected. "I do between five and ten ceremonies a year."

"I take it they're not your favorite jobs."

"I've planned dozens of weddings over my career, but only a handful of the couples I worked with are still married. Planning charity events is my true passion, but with the recent slump in the economy those assignments are few and far between."

"The tourism industry has been hit hard, too." To steer her in the right direction, he placed a hand on her back. A thousand volts of desire tore through her. Claudia wondered if he had felt *it,* too, but didn't see a change in his demeanor. Her eyes targeted his mouth, then spilled over the smooth contours of his chest and down his waist. Goose bumps pricked her skin, and lust ignited between her legs.

Claudia tore her gaze away from his face and ordered her horny body into submission. The last time she'd been this taken with someone she'd…she'd… The truth stunned her. This was a first. Thoughts of kissing him and caressing him bombarded her mind. Then the video playing in her head turned X-rated. She saw them sharing fiery French kisses, saw them ripping off each other's clothes. Was he a slow, tender lover? Or a five-minute man? She'd never entertained the thought of having a one-night stand, but the energy radiating between them was intense, and the stress of the last three weeks had finally caught up to her. Her body needed a release, but having sex with the hunky resort manager wasn't the answer. Right?

Claudia grabbed ahold of herself. This wasn't a shared attraction. It was a one-sided nuisance, that's what it was. And she'd deal with it the best way she knew how—by ignoring it. But when Santiago lowered his hand so that it now rested comfortably on the small of her back, Claudia knew staying away from him would be easier said than done.

Chapter 6

"If this is a dream, *please* don't wake me up!"

Claudia knew Santiago was standing behind her, but she couldn't stop gushing over the lavish, two-thousand-square-foot apartment. With its open-concept floor plan and warm color scheme the suite flowed easily from one room to the next. Decorated with designer fabrics and stunning furniture, it resembled a celebrity home she'd once seen featured in *Architectural Digest* magazine. The apartment reeked of grandeur but looked as serene as a country cottage.

"I take it you like the suite."

"Like it? I love it! The turquoise walls are calming, the burgundy accessories are a brilliant touch and the watercolor paintings open the room right up."

Santiago chuckled. "Were you an interior designer in another life?"

"No, but I worked at a design company for a year and learned a few things." Claudia drew her hand along the back of the couch. "You don't have to be Martha Stewart to know what looks good and what doesn't. You just have to think outside the box."

"I'm hopeless when it comes to decorating," he confessed, wearing a wry smile. "That's why I paid a professional to furnish my home."

"I thought you lived here at the resort."

"I do, but I also have a small property in my hometown." Santiago didn't know why he felt compelled to lie. There was nothing 'small' about his estate, or the custom-made garage that housed his collection of European sports cars. Located in an upscale neighborhood nicknamed Luxury Row, the six-bedroom house stretched across two acres and carried a five-million-dollar price tag. But he wasn't about to tell Claudia that. At least not yet. "I only purchased it a few months ago."

"The resort must pay you very well."

He heard the accusation in her voice, saw the doubt in her eyes.

"It's not much, just a place to lay my head." Santiago cringed at the sound of his voice. He was talking faster than an auctioneer, and his nose was twitching like he was about to sneeze. "Veracruz is an hour away, so I only go home on the weekends. I enjoy my new place, but I prefer staying here. There's so much to do. And our champagne brunch is the best around."

Her lips turned down at the corners. "That sounds expensive *and* indulgent."

"It is, but it's worth it. And it can be served poolside or in the comfort of your suite."

"I rarely drink, and never before noon."

"Then come down to the Oasis restaurant and we'll have pancakes."

Claudia squinted, furrowing her eyebrows as if she was considering his offer. But she wasn't. Not when she had a sleek, gourmet kitchen stocked with supplies. Besides, hanging out at the resort was risky. American tourists were crawling all over the place, and she hadn't traveled two thousand miles only to be discovered by someone following William's case. "I'll think about it."

"And I'll save you a seat."

The allure of his smile made her melt like a bag of ice cubes left out in the desert. An unstoppable force with innate charm, Santiago Medina not only radiated positive energy, he oozed with a charisma that few men his age possessed.

Claudia climbed the steps and threw open the French doors. The postcard-perfect view was breathtaking, the most spectacular thing she had ever seen. Millions of stars glittered in the sky, tropical fish caused ripples in the emerald-blue water, and the towering mountain peaks in the distance enhanced the mystical scene. The breeze kept the air cool and ruffled the sails on the boats drifting into the harbor. A giant wave rushed up the shore, causing the teenagers strolling along the beach to run for cover. "I bet there are some incredible trails around here."

"You're right, there are. We offer guided tours that range from thirty-minute strolls to intense three-hour excursions twice a day," he explained. "If you want, I could add your name to the list of hikers heading out on the beginner trail in the morning."

"No, thanks, I'd much rather go alone. I'm a seasoned hiker, and I don't want anyone slowing me down."

"The trails are steep, and we're expecting record-breaking temperatures tomorrow. To be on the safe side, you should hike with a partner. What time do you want to start?"

Claudia almost laughed out loud when the resort manager volunteered his services. *Men are so predictable,* she thought, shaking her head. "I'd like to head out at sunrise."

Santiago coughed. "Wow, that's early."

"You must be a late riser."

"Guilty as charged. I'm a bear in the mornings, but I'd still like to accompany you on that hike. I know all six trail routes, and the hidden treasures in and around the Baja…"

Enraptured by the smooth texture of his voice, she listened intently as he described the panoramic mountain views and the magic of the cascading waterfalls. The man had perfect everything—teeth, skin, hair—and although he was attractive enough to rock the runway he seemed like a genuine, down-to-earth guy. Indulging in a summer fling would be reckless, as dangerous as hang-gliding without a parachute, but if Claudia was ever in the market for a lover Santiago Medina would be her first choice. "Don't take this the wrong way, but I was really looking forward to going alone."

"Then I'll keep my distance," he said, a grin caressing his lips. "I'll stay a mile back."

Claudia hated how he used his smile as a weapon, flashing it whenever he wanted to put her at ease or lighten the mood. What struck her was how well it worked. Every time he showed those pearly whites, her defenses crumbled. It wasn't safe to be around him. Not with those superstar looks and that disarming grin. Fighting their attraction was hard enough, and she feared what would happen if they were alone in the woods. She'd probably be so busy checking him out, she'd wipe out on the trail and twist her ankle.

"Let's meet in front of the building."

His eyes pulled her in, made her lower her guard and forget her plans to keep her distance. Claudia didn't want Santiago to accompany her, but how would it look if she shot him down? But for his generosity, she'd be sleeping in the lobby, smack-dab beside the kissing couples. "All right. 6:00 a.m. sharp."

"Great, it's a dat—" He stopped midword and nodded instead. "I'll be there."

Picking up one of the brochures on the desk, she scanned the cover and marveled at the various services the resort offered. The Sea of Cortez Resort had everything a tourist could want. A drug store, three restaurants, a bank. It was a gem of a hotel, and the next time Claudia saw Maxine she was going to give her a big, fat kiss. "I've stayed in a lot of nice hotels, but this resort takes the cake. I've never seen—" Claudia broke off when she heard a knock on the door.

"I hope you don't mind, but I took the liberty of ordering you dinner. Airline food leaves much to be desired, and I suspect you passed on the pot roast and green salad."

"How did you know?"

"Because I passed on it, too!" Santiago gave a hearty laugh. Opening the door, he greeted the lanky waiter and wheeled the food cart into the living room.

The piquant scent filling the air incited Claudia's hunger. "Something smells heavenly," she said, inhaling the aroma.

Santiago whipped off the cover with a flourish. "Since it's late, and I wasn't sure if you liked Mexican food, I had the chef prepare a hearty vegetarian chili with fresh pan bread. For dessert you'll have the richest, creamiest cheesecake ever made."

"Thank you. You've been most kind."

"Is there anything else I can get for you before I leave?"

"You're not staying?" Claudia heard the disappointment in her voice and cleared her throat. "This is a lot of food, and I doubt I'll be able to finish it all."

"I wish I could stay, but my mom is making a special dinner tonight and I promised her I'd be there." Santiago gestured with his index finger to the door. "I'm at the end of the hall, in Suite 1170, so if you have any questions or concerns feel free to give me a call."

"Or, I could just phone the front desk."

"The staff here is great, but they operate on island time and—"

"Island time? Does that mean they're always running late?"

"Not on purpose. The attitude in Cabo is 'things get done when they get done,' and no one ever feels the need to rush, especially here at the resort."

"That doesn't bother me," she told him. "I prefer to do things for myself anyway."

"Like carry your own luggage."

Claudia smothered a smile. Gazing outside the balcony window, she allowed her thoughts to drift like the tide rolling onto the shore. "Is the city center walking distance from here?"

"Yes, but it will probably take you close to an hour." His eyebrows drew together, creating twin peaks, but he spoke in a soft tone. "We have a gift shop and a drugstore on the main floor. I'm sure you'll find everything you're looking for there."

"This is a lovely resort, but I want to see Mexico and experience the culture firsthand. Attending cultural events and perusing the outdoor markets are on the top of my to-do list."

"It sounds like you have your whole trip mapped out."

"I'm an event planner," she said with a shrug. "That's what I do."

"We can talk more about your itinerary tomorrow during our hike."

"That would be great. And thanks again for everything."

He gave a small nod, then strode out of the suite.

Careful not to trip over her luggage, she shot across the room and cracked open the door. *I'm just making sure he's gone,* she told herself, sticking her head into the hall. *Female travelers can never be too careful these days.* Her gaze zeroed in on Santiago's butt, and her knees went weak. Did the man ever have a body on him. Wide shoulders, a hard, broad chest, and arms that looked strong enough to scoop her up and carry her to his—

Claudia struck down the thought but continued her rearview appraisal of the sexy resort manager. Santiago had perfect posture and moved with confidence, but not in a way that turned her off. Too bad, because when it came to weeding out the good guys from the jerks, she was as clueless as a nun with a vibrator.

A brunette in a leopard-print bikini turned the corner and sashayed down the hall as if she was on the Miss Universe stage. Santiago strode past her. He didn't stop or sneak a look as she passed by. Claudia couldn't believe it. And neither could the brunette. Shock covered her face, and a scowl crimped her lips.

Claudia closed her gaping mouth. There was more to this Santiago guy than met the eye, and that worried her. She wondered if what he'd told her about his plans for tonight was true. He was having dinner with his mom on a Friday night? That was hard to believe. But who cared? He was the resort manager, not her love interest. That was why she'd agreed to go hiking with him. Santiago was harmless, safe. And Claudia liked that he was a regular guy. Not a loud, arrogant executive who thought he was the salt of the earth.

Her eyes slipped down his physique. Santiago Medina put the *f* in fine, but that didn't mean she was interested in him. She wasn't, only curious why such a hot guy was still on the market. Or was he? He could have a harem of baby mamas, an on-again, off-again love waiting in the wings, or a sex buddy stashed away at the resort. In light of what she'd learned about her ex in recent weeks, nothing about Santiago would surprise her.

Feeling guilty for spying, she stepped away from the door and returned to the living room. Claudia didn't know what to do first: eat, unpack or take a shower. But when she remembered the fiasco that had happened during check-in, she grabbed her travel bag, took out her laptop and plugged it in. Hopefully, she'd be able to access her credit card online and fix the problem. While she waited for her home page to load, she sampled the food Santiago had ordered. The vegetarian chili was rich and flavorful, and by the time she logged into her email, she'd finished the main course.

Claudia scooped up the dessert and settled onto the couch. She had three new messages, and they all had the same subject line: My 2013 Wedding. A groan rumbled in the back of her throat. Three more weddings? That brought the grand total to twelve. Planning five summer weddings would be the death of her, but she couldn't afford to be picky about jobs. Not when her accounts were frozen and she was strapped for cash.

The third message was from someone named Jeanette Miller, and the tone of her email was friendly, jovial, as if they'd known each other all their lives. The name tickled her memory, but it wasn't until she finished reading the message that she remembered the petite Atlanta native who'd served as the maid of honor at Damien and Niveah's wedding. Now, the love-struck couple was expecting their first child, and Claudia was thrilled for them.

Thinking about the grand, over-the-top bash she'd orchestrated last summer made Claudia smile. Over the course of her twelve-year career, she'd planned hundreds of weddings, and even a handful of silver anniversary parties, but she'd never seen a couple more in love. Their tender, impromptu kiss at the altar before exchanging vows had moved the audience to tears. It was a magical, enchanted night, one she'd labored tirelessly to achieve, and Damien had been so impressed with her work he'd hired her to plan his company's winter charity ball. Claudia couldn't wait to begin, and once the media storm surrounding William quieted down, she'd throw herself into the project.

A new email popped into her inbox. Hopeful it was another job, Claudia clicked on the message. But when she read the first line, her blood ran cold.

I've lost everything because of you—my job, my marriage, my house—and mark my words, Mrs. Prescott, I'm going to make you and *your thieving husband pay.*

Scared the laptop would implode, she pushed it aside and

leapt to her feet. The thought was ludicrous, as absurd as her decision to marry William after a brief, six-month courtship, but she backed away from the couch anyway.

Wrapping her arms around her shoulders, she held herself tightly and concentrated on slowing her breathing. It felt like someone was holding a pillow over her face. Claudia stared outside and fixed her gaze on the vivid crescent moon. The voices in her head grew so loud she couldn't ignore them. Who was the message from? An angry investor or that crazed, wild-eyed man who'd confronted her outside of her office?

Closing her eyes didn't block out the memory of last week's chilling encounter. Instead, the darkness put her back in Richmond, back on that busy, high-traffic street. If she'd been paying attention, she would have seen the disheveled man emerge from the alley, but she'd been lost in her own world, and by the time he snuck up on her she had nowhere to hide. He said she owed him, said that because of what William did he'd lost his life savings.

"I'm deeply sorry about what my *ex*-husband did," she began, embarrassed that they'd attracted a small crowd, "but I had absolutely nothing to do with—"

That's as far as she got.

"You rich bitch!" The man dug his bony fingers into her shoulders. His rancid, onion breath burned her eyes. Bile thickened the walls of her throat, trapping her screams. Delirious with fear, Claudia felt her legs buckle and groped for something to break her fall. *This can't be happening to me! Not at my place of business!*

Terror struck, leaving her scared, dizzy and battling nausea. The man shook her with such rage, she dropped to the cold, hard pavement. Claudia felt like she was living out a scene in a gruesome slasher movie, and the worst part was, she was too scared to fight back.

Sympathetic bystanders rushed to her aid, but not before the man vowed to make her pay. Claudia could still hear the animosity in his voice, could still see the violent, angry lines wrinkling his forehead and cheeks. The man wasn't making idle threats, and Claudia had no intention of being around when he returned to finish her off.

That incident, plus the onslaught of media attention, were why she'd skipped town.

To calm her nerves, Claudia drew a slow, deep breath and exhaled through her nose. She wanted to talk to someone about how she was feeling, and surprisingly, it was Santiago Medina who came to mind. Confiding in him was out of the question, but having his company would be nice. She was alone, in a foreign country, and she needed a shoulder to cry on. And Santiago had a toned, muscular set of arms that she'd love to have around her.

Spotting her cell phone on the wet bar, she crossed the room and scooped it up. It rang, shattering the eerie silence in the suite. Claudia sighed in relief. It had to be Max. Her sister was the only person who called this late, and despite arguing earlier, she was anxious to speak to her. "Great timing, Max. I *really* need to talk."

"Hello. This is a collect call from the Richmond County Jail," said an automated female voice. "To accept the call and all subsequent charges please press one."

Claudia was shaking so hard, she had to hold the phone with both hands. Her pulse throbbed in her ears, and her tongue was so slick, so heavy with fear, she couldn't speak.

"I am sorry, but I did not hear your response. To accept the call—"

Claudia clicked off the phone and hurled it at the couch. Why couldn't William leave her alone? Hadn't he caused her enough pain?

Her laptop beeped, and the AOL Messenger announced that she had six new messages.

Staring at the computer, her fists clenched at her sides, she wondered if the emails were from a client, an enemy or William. Did inmates have access to computers? Claudia frowned. Did it matter? Her ex was resourceful, skilled at throwing around his weight and bullying others. Hadn't he proved that repeatedly during their ten-year marriage?

Resentment burned in her chest like heartburn. He'd destroyed her hopes and dreams for the future, but still had the nerve to call her collect from jail. William's arrogance shouldn't have surprised her. He thought the sun rose and set for his pleasure, and that she'd been put on this earth to do his bidding. He belittled her, insulted her and thought nothing of embarrassing her in public. But instead of standing up to him and demanding he treat her with respect, she took everything he dished out. Aside from her sister, William was the only family she had and Claudia had been determined to make it work, even at the expense of her pride.

Then, she'd discovered that she was pregnant.

And her marriage, which was already hanging on by a thread, went from bad to worse.

Chapter 7

"**I**'ve done a lot of stupid things in my life, but this takes the cake!" Claudia grumbled, hauling her aching body up the steep, winding path. The forest was inundated with the scent of poinsettias and scarlet blossoms, but the soothing fragrance did nothing to calm her. Claudia hurt in places she couldn't reach and was staggering along the trail like a drunk after happy hour. "This is torture! I can't take anymore!"

Pressing her lips together to trap a groan, she cleaned the sweat off her forehead with her pink wristbands. Her sunglasses skated down her nose, and for the third time in seconds she pushed them back in place. She wanted to kick something—hard—but as she grumbled about her growing list of aches and pains, she realized she had no one to blame for her misery but herself. Hadn't Santiago warned her not to go off alone? An image of the resort manager with the big heart and powerfully built body filled her mind. Claudia shivered and felt her heart quicken two beats. *Why does that keep happening?* she wondered, shaking her head and all thoughts of Santiago from her mind.

They were supposed to meet at sunrise, but after tossing and turning all night, she'd slipped out of bed, dressed, and set off at the first light of day. That threatening email and William's phone call from the county jail had left her spooked and had convinced her that Santiago Medina was just one more problem she didn't need. Maybe he was, maybe he wasn't, but her track record with the opposite sex was pitiful, and after a disastrous failed marriage, she didn't trust her instincts. Keeping her distance from men, especially sweet guys like Santiago, was definitely the safer, smarter choice.

So, why do I feel guilty for blowing him off?

Sunshine and fresh air was the perfect antidote for stress, but after an hour on this steep death trap Claudia was ready to quit. This course was for athletic thrill seekers, not regular people like her, and if she didn't get down soon she'd be leaving on a stretcher.

Short of breath and scared she was going to fall headfirst into the cacti if she took another step, Claudia rested against a tall shady tree and fanned her face. Butterflies danced around her, flapping their wings to the tranquil sounds of the forest. With views of the ocean, the rich landscape and bubbling streams, she was standing in the ideal place to admire the natural beauty of the peninsula. The sun was so luminous and bright that it didn't look real. Large, colorful birds twittered the season's song, crickets danced in the air and the sound of the rushing waterfall made Claudia momentarily forget the shooting pains in her lower calves.

Down below, on a long stretch of powdery white sand, twentysomethings played Frisbee, tanned on chaise loungers and tackled giant waves on their towering boogie boards. Silver-haired guests reclined in posh, white cabanas, while waiters hustled around refreshing their drinks and serving appetizers.

Hoping to see beyond the beach, Claudia stepped out from behind the tree. The bar came into view, and so did Santiago Medina. He was hard to miss. With his wavy hair blowing in the wind and that statue-worthy physique, he stood out from the crowd like the world's tallest man at a little-people convention. And not just because of his looks. Most of the men swaggered around, using their puny, puffed-out chests to attract attention, but not Santiago. He was fully dressed and looked great in his navy shirt and loose-fitting white pants. Leaning against the bar, holding a glass tumbler, he looked debonair and cool without even trying. *He's wasting his talents working here,* she thought, loving the privacy her location provided. *He should be in movies, sharing that disarming smile with the world.*

Claudia glanced at her watch. She'd been stuck on this mountain for ninety minutes? The phone call she'd received last night left her so scattered, she'd forgotten to do her online banking, and Claudia wanted to have her credit card situation straightened out before the resort staff came looking for her.

Though I wouldn't mind if Santiago was the one who came knocking on my door.

At the thought, her skin flushed with heat. Smiling ruefully, she took one last look at the bar and then stepped back onto the trail. Claudia came upon a clearing in the forest and spotted a female hiker descending the mountain. Dressed in candy-apple-red workout gear—complete with matching head and wristbands—the older woman looked like the Mexican version of Jane Fonda. And to keep the hiker in her sights, Claudia had to do a slow jog. The woman was obviously an experienced hiker because she was zooming up the hill like it was nobody's business. *I must be in worse shape than I thought!*

The peaceful sound of the rushing stream made Claudia feel even more lethargic. Licking the dryness from her lips, she considered stopping for a drink. Was the water safe? With her luck, she'd get sick and end up spending the rest of her vacation in the hospital. As if she could afford a hospital bill; she couldn't even cover the cost of the incidentals in her suite!

Staring longingly at the stream, she tried to talk herself out of dipping her face into the stream and having her fill. *I'll just have a sip,* Claudia decided. *One little sip won't kill me.* She'd finished her water bottle ten minutes into the hike, but if she'd known the terrain was as rugged as the Grand Canyon she would have packed the kitchen sink.

Claudia doubled over, dropped her hands on her knees and waited for the burning sensation in her chest to subside. Her arms were on fire, her legs ached and sweat was trickling furiously down her cheeks. Claudia pictured herself back in the comfort of her luxury suite. The first thing she was going to do when she returned home was soak in a tub filled with Bengay. If that didn't ease the knots in her back, she'd treat herself to an in-suite massage. A rubdown, from a guy with strong arms, was just what the doctor ordered.

Santiago's obviously a man with hidden talents, she thought, feeling the heat that was in her chest spread south. *I bet he could soothe the aches in my—*

A spine-chilling scream shattered the morning silence.

Claudia's head whipped up. Spotting the female hiker on the ground, she sprinted through the meadow and crouched down beside her.

The woman's eyebrows merged together. Dirt smudged her cheeks, and twigs were poking out of her thick, ash-brown hair. She was breathing heavily, rapidly, as if each breath was a fight. *"Hola. ¿Cómo está?"* said Claudia, fumbling to recall her Spanish.

A look of relief washed over the woman's thin, oval face. *"Estoy bien, pero pienso que puedo haber torcido el tobillo. Tropecé en...."*

Claudia was listening intently, but found herself distracted by the woman's animated hand gestures. Add to that, she was speaking a mile a minute. What was the word for *help* again? *"Soy norteamericana."*

"You're American?"

Claudia smiled sheepishly. "As you can see, my Spanish isn't very good."

"And neither is my English!" Soft lines kissed her mouth when she laughed, but she had radiant skin and a slender frame. "I'm sorry I startled you. I slipped on a rock, but I'm okay."

"Do you need some help?"

"No, all I need is a moment to catch my breath."

"If you don't mind, I'll just take a quick look at your ankle." Resting the woman's foot on her lap, she untied her laces and slowly removed her cross-trainer sneakers. "There's no swelling, but that doesn't mean it isn't broken."

"It feels okay," she said, rotating her foot.

Claudia slid the woman's sneaker back on.

"Thanks for stopping to check on me. That was very thoughtful of you."

"It's no problem. If the roles were reversed, I'm sure you'd do the same for me."

Squinting, her gaze as strong and intense as the sun's blinding rays, the woman tilted her head up. "I know your face," she said. "I can't remember where I've seen you before though."

Panic choked Claudia's windpipes. Had the collapse of Qwest Capital Investments gone worldwide? Was her picture in the local newspaper? Turning away, she lowered her eyes to the ground and pretended to be studying the granite rocks scattered along the trail.

"You're that actress! Halle something-or-other."

Releasing the breath she'd had trapped in her lungs, she smiled sheepishly and ruffled her bangs with her fingertips. "The only thing Halle Berry and I have in common are our short hairstyles and a series of failed relationships."

"My *abuela* was married five times, and she used to say, 'The more beautiful the woman, the more unlucky she is in love!'"

"I'm hardly beautiful."

"You must not have mirrors at home!" A smile touched her lips. "You're slim and youthful and have a warm aura."

"Thirty might be the new twenty in Hollywood, but I feel every one of my years," Claudia quipped, massaging the tenderness in her legs. "And that brutal hike didn't help any!"

"I know just how you feel. Every time I watch an episode of the *Real Housewives of Guadalajara* I feel ancient! Getting old is terrible, and worse still, my husband won't let me go under the knife to fix what's wrong!"

Claudia laughed. After only a few minutes in the woman's presence, she felt comfortable, at ease. The hiker's fun-loving, feel-good persona made her think of Aunt Hattie and all the good times they'd shared. "Don't be so hard on yourself. I think you look great. You have the figure of a teenager and not a wrinkle in sight."

"Thank you." Her hazel eyes twinkled when she smiled. "I've been talking your ear off, but I don't even know your name. I'm Ana."

"Claudia."

"What part of the States are you from?"

"The South." Claudia liked Ana, but she didn't feel comfortable divulging personal information. To deflect attention from herself, she steered the conversation back to Ana. "I bet your grandkids just adore you. You're so energetic and full of life."

The light in her eyes dimmed. "No grandkids yet. My daughter passed away two years ago, and despite my best efforts my son refuses to settle down."

"I am so sorry for your loss."

Ana dabbed at the corners of her eyes, then raised her head toward the sky. "Marisol probably would have had three or four kids by now. She always wanted a big family, and she would have been an incredible mother."

A long, cumbersome silence followed.

Using a rock as leverage, Ana pressed her hands against it and pushed herself up. Pain streaked across her face and a groan shot out of her mouth.

"Do you need my help?"

Ana waved off the offer with a flick of her hand. "I'm fine. I think I may have tweaked my ankle, but after a couple aspirin and a shot of tequila, I'll be as good as new!"

"There's a home remedy I've never heard of. Tell me, does the aspirin-tequila trick cure back pain, too? I'm so sore it hurts to move."

"This must be your first time on Cardiac Mountain."

"What a suitable nickname," she joked, a smirk teasing her lips. "I don't think I'll be hiking this trail again. I came to Cabo to relax, not to torture myself."

"These trails are harder than they look, and I see banged-up tourists like you at least once a day. Bathe in chamomile tonight, and you'll be fit to tango in the morning!"

Claudia laughed. "You must hike a lot."

"Every morning, seven days a week."

"Wow, that's dedication."

"I like to get my workout in before the day gets crazy. I'm in the hospitality business, and since my husband's away a lot, I have to oversee the day-to-day operations of the family business alone. I love what I do, but it's a lot of work!"

"I know just what you mean. I have my own business as well, and some days I'm so busy running around I don't even have time to eat."

Ana laughed. "I *wish* I had that problem!"

Claudia watched Ana. Her movements were unsteady, and she was huffing and puffing like a sprinter powering across the finish line.

"I don't think I can finish the trail," she confessed, staring at her leg. "If it's not too much trouble, could you use your cell phone and call my son? I left mine at home—"

"I can help you."

Her face was wrinkled with doubt. "But you're just an itty-bitty thing."

"I'm a lot stronger than I look. We'll go slow and stop whenever you need a break."

"Are you staying nearby? I'd hate to put you out of your way."

"I'm staying at the Sea of Cortez Resort," she told her.

"What a small world. So am I!" Ana laughed. "Tell me, what do you think of the resort?"

"It's incredible. Unlike anything I've ever seen. And the resort manager has been so kind and gracious. If not for his help last night, I would have had to stay somewhere else."

Beaming brighter than a ten-carat diamond, she clasped her hands together like a mother silently applauding her child. "Ramón *is* great, isn't he? He's the heart and soul of the—"

"I haven't met him yet. I was referring to the other guy, Santiago Medina."

"Santiago?"

A smile crept over Claudia's lips. "We met at the airport lounge in Washington, then ended up on the same plane headed to Cabo."

"Santiago?" Ana looked bewildered, but nodded and smiled. "Yes, of course, Santiago, the *other* resort manager."

"He escorted me to my suite and was kind enough to order dinner for me as well."

Ana's mouth fell open. "You don't say?"

"You seem surprised."

"Not at all. You seem to have a good head on your shoulders and you have great, positive energy. It's no wonder my…" She coughed, rubbed a hand over her chest as if she had a serious case of heartburn. "I'm not surprised that Santiago's interested in you. In many ways, you're just his type. Tall, fit, curvy."

"He's not interested in me romantically," she insisted, ignoring the butterflies pelting her stomach at the thought of the dreamy resort manager liking her. "He was just doing his job."

"I think he went above and beyond." Ana lowered her gaze to Claudia's left hand. "I find it hard to believe that a pretty young thing like you doesn't have a lot of male admirers. Or a boyfriend back home in the States anxiously awaiting your return."

A scowl curled the corners of Claudia's lips. "Men are trouble, and I could do without every last one of them."

"Santiago's not the typical Mexican guy. He's sensitive, open-minded and a man of incredible faith. You'd be hard-pressed to find someone better."

"You know a lot about him. Do you work at the resort as well?"

Ana sideswiped the question. "You *do* find him attractive, don't you?"

In her haste to deny the charge, Claudia tripped over her tongue. "I don't know." It was a whopper of a lie, but what else was she supposed to say? Admitting to this woman— and herself—that she was attracted to the sexy resort manager was out of the question.

"What do you mean, you don't know? Either you do or you don't."

"I haven't taken a good look at him."

"Sure you haven't." Ana waved Claudia over and hooked a hand through her arm. "Be a dear and escort me back to the resort. I just remembered there's something important I have to do, and time is of the essence!"

Chapter 8

Santiago threw down his pen and watched as it skidded off the mahogany desk. Now he knew why his mother had asked him to meet with Ramón to review the renovation budget. And why she was absent. Balancing the books was a long, painstaking task, and after crunching the numbers for hours there was no end to his suffering in sight. He'd rather be back outside, hanging out at the bar with his friends. Or with Claudia. Thinking about her and how she'd ditched him that morning made a grin curl his lips. Getting even with the sly Southern belle was on the top of his to-do-list, but first he had to finish the task at hand. "It doesn't matter what I do, I still end up hundreds of thousands of dollars in the red."

Ramón stared at the spreadsheets on the desk, but didn't speak.

Santiago gestured to the financial statements. "Either the numbers are wrong or someone's been using the account as their own private piggy bank. We made a sixteen percent profit last year, but half of it is gone."

The resort manager glanced around the office as if it was his first time in the room.

"Where is the money, Ramón? The builders will be finished at the end of the month, and they're expecting to be paid in full."

"Yo no sé."

"You don't know? But you're the resort manager. If you don't know, who does?"

Ramón shifted around on his chair like he had ants in his khaki pants. Mumbling to himself in Spanish, he fiddled with the knot on his tangerine tie.

"I want to know what's going on around here, and I want to know now."

Nothing. Not a blink, not a scowl, not a fiery, passionate denial.

"Have you been dipping into the bank accounts?"

A look of horror flashed in his eyes. *"Dijo que me podría despedir si dije algo."*

"Who's 'he'?" Deep down, Santiago knew who the culprit was, but he wanted to hear what the manager had to say. Only four people had access to the resort's bank accounts, but only one bullied and threatened the employees. "Who said he'd can you?"

Ramón grabbed his mug then chugged a mouthful of coffee. *"Se padre."*

A growing sense of dread filled Santiago. His deepest fears had been realized and were now playing out in his mind like a real-life nightmare. Remembering that Ramón was more comfortable speaking in his native language, he said in Spanish, "Tell me exactly what my father said."

Ramón's shoulders collapsed. After what seemed like an hour, he slowly recounted the conversation he'd had with his boss weeks earlier. His voice was tight, constricted, but he told his story with more flair than a seasoned crime writer.

It took a moment for Santiago to process what the resort

manager said. He didn't know the middle-aged man well, but he believed him. His father had strong-armed Ramón into withdrawing two hundred thousand dollars from the resort's accounts and threatened to fire him if he talked. It wasn't the first time his dad had siphoned funds from the business, but it was definitely going to be the last. "Did he say what he needed the money for?"

"Dijo que la estación en Acapulco no hace dinero y él debe pagar sus préstamos."

Stroking his chin, he considered what Ramón shared. *It's possible he needed the money to cover the bills at the Acapulco resort, but why not go through the proper channels? Why keep secrets from me and Mom?*

"¿Qué haremos ahora?"

That was a good question. What *were* they going to do? The resort was hemorrhaging money, and if he didn't put a stop to it there would be nothing left. And where would that leave his mom? He'd disappointed her in the past, but not this time. Confronting his father would have to wait until he returned from Acapulco. This was not something to discuss over the phone, and since they hadn't spoken in months, waiting a few more weeks wouldn't make much of a difference. The fantasy suites would be completed by the end of the month, but it wasn't too late to trim costs. He'd worked miracles at larger companies, and he'd do it again at his parents' business.

"Let's look at these numbers again." Energized by his thoughts, he pulled his chair closer to the table and reexamined the spread sheets. "There are several areas where we can trim costs, without spoiling the integrity of the project. For example, using standard, low-emissivity windows instead of custom-made coverings will save us twenty grand."

"Good thinking." The resort manager nodded and tapped a fat index finger on the last column. "We'd save even more money if we fired that snooty event coordinator your mother hired last week. During the consultation, she flicked a finger at me and demanded I fetch more ice cubes for her lemonade. I have never been more insulted!"

Santiago was laughing on the inside, but he wore a sympathetic face. "I'm sure she didn't mean anything by it, Ramón. Mrs. Ortega has a lot on her plate right now. She's designing the destination wedding packages, as well as planning the celebration bash."

"I have a feeling Miss High and Mighty is going to be a royal pain in the butt."

"How much is she costing us?" Santiago asked, tapping his fingers absently on the desk.

"Twenty-five thousand dollars."

"That sounds reasonable to me. After all, she's—"

Ramón broke in. "That's what she's charging us *per week.*"

"What?" The word shot out of his mouth. "That's highway robbery! No wonder the renovation budget is skyrocketing through the roof."

A scowl wrinkled Ramón's face. "I think she's ripping us off, but your mom is a huge fan of her work. Apparently, this Ortega woman has good aurora or something." He frowned, shrugged his shoulders. "At least I think that's what your mother said. I can't quite remember."

Oh, brother. Not this again. Having her palm read last year at the Cervantes Festival had turned his sane, practical mother into an energy-loving nut. To ward off evil spirits, she'd moved around the furniture, plastered framed quotes on the walls and beautified the desk with photos. Santiago thought the office was crowded, packed tighter than a socialite's suitcase, but the hand-painted pottery and scented candles did give the space a warm, welcoming feel.

"I don't have a problem paying for a job well done, but planning parties isn't rocket science. I bet if we looked around we could find someone more affordable."

"But your mom has already hired her."

"Then, I'll be the one to fire her."

"Santiago, it's too late in the game to be making huge changes," Ramón said, scratching at the stubble on his chin. "Mrs. Ortega is flying in on Wednesday morning from Monterrey."

"Then, that gives us three days to find a suitable replacement." His gaze strayed to the open window, and the sweet scent of the afternoon breeze made Santiago think about Claudia. She was probably in her suite, luxuriating on the balcony with a magazine and a fruity cocktail. Or maybe she was working in the office on that winter charity ball she'd mentioned earlier—

Santiago bolted upright in his chair.

That was it!

Excited about the idea taking shape in his mind, he realized he'd just found the answer to his problem. He'd hire Claudia! She had experience, was as thrifty as the Grinch and wouldn't treat the budget like her personal wish list.

"I don't feel good about this," Ramón grumbled, dragging a hand over his head. "And Señora Medina is going to be angry when she learns that you axed her favorite event coordinator."

Santiago patted his shoulder. "Have some faith. I know what I'm doing."

"But Mrs. Ortega is the best in the business and a personal friend of your mother's. If she doesn't plan the celebration bash, who will?"

A Southern belle with a keen eye for detail and the best pair of legs in all of Cabo. Hiring Claudia would not only save the resort money, it would give him an opportunity to get to know her better. And that was a definite bonus.

Standing, he smoothed a hand over his hair and adjusted his shirt collar.

"Where are you going?" Ramón asked, his bushy eyebrows jammed together in a crooked line. "We have to find a replacement for Mrs. Ortega today, Santiago. That reporter woman from *Good Morning Cabo* is doing a feature on the resort next month, and we have a lot of interviews and radio spots planned to promote the celebration bash."

"Leave everything to me," he announced, already halfway through the office.

"Do you want me to go online and make a list of all the local event coordinators?"

Santiago grinned. "Nope. I already have someone in mind."

Hobbling like a ninety-year-old woman with a broken cane, Claudia pushed open the door to her posh suite and collapsed onto the closest thing with four legs. Seven hours ago she'd set off for a relaxing stroll in the mountains, but instead of basking in the sunshine, she'd ended up aggravating every bone in her body. The only bright spot of the day had been meeting Ana. At the thought of the older woman, Claudia smiled. She had been anxious to return to her suite, but Ana wouldn't let her leave. At least not until they'd had lunch. Two aspirins and a shot of tequila later, and the older woman was flittering around the kitchen, reheating leftovers and setting the table.

"What do you think of the tortilla shells?" she asked, pouring peach lemonade into Claudia's oversize glass. "I've never used flax seed before, but I'm trying to adopt a healthier lifestyle, and my dietician said it's good for me."

Claudia chewed until every muscle in her jaw hurt, then forced the rubbery bread down her throat. It tasted like something cooked in an Easy-Bake Oven, but she smiled and told her hostess it was delicious. Hurting others had never been her style, and she could never understand why her ex-husband enjoyed putting people down. He garnered a sick satisfaction in berating her, and when he'd unleashed his full terror on her last Christmas Eve, she'd feared for her life. *I should have left when I had the chance,* she thought, replaying the events of that night in her mind for the hundredth time. *If I had followed my instincts, I'd still be...*

Feelings of despair overwhelmed her, spread from her heart to her soul like an infectious disease. To keep the tears stinging the back of her eyes at bay, Claudia remembered how much fun she'd had that morning. Ana was a hoot. Sixty years young with a sharp mind and a killer wit. During lunch, they'd chatted about celebrity gossip and Mexican culture, and before Claudia knew it two hours had flown by. Being with Ana made Claudia feel good, energized, the way she used to feel before her life took a disastrous turn for the worse. Claudia couldn't remember the last time she'd laughed so hard, and when Ana suggested they have breakfast again tomorrow morning, she'd readily agreed. Why not? Spending time with Ana would take her mind off the fraud case and the seriously sexy resort manager with the ripped physique.

Craving a cold drink, she licked her lips and stared longingly at the wet bar. Ana swore by her unconventional pain remedy, but Claudia needed more than some aspirin and a shot of tequila to revive her. *A defibrillator would do the trick.* Claudia wished she had the strength to get up, but she was so utterly exhausted she couldn't move.

"Hello? Claudia?"

At the sound of the deep masculine voice she'd heard last night in her dreams, Claudia bolted upright. When she saw Santiago standing in the doorway, the wall lights illuminating his delicious silhouette, she almost fell off her chair. Seeing Santiago was the ultimate adrenaline rush, and his charming grin caused desire to spark between her legs.

Avoiding his gaze, she combed her fingertips through the ends of her matted hair. She looked a mess, smelled like funk, and had so many blisters on her feet a searing pain shot through her side when she sprang to her feet. Hoping he'd keep his distance, but doubtful he would, she slid behind the couch. Right, as if a physical barrier would conceal her hideous scent.

"It's good to see you." His greeting was warm, friendly, as if he'd been looking forward to seeing her all day. "The resort is safe, but I still wouldn't recommend leaving your door open. You never know who might be lurking around."

"I thought I'd closed it, but I was so out of it when I came in, I didn't double-check."

"Are you okay? You look a little worse for wear."

"Let's just say I won't be hiking on Cardiac Mountain anytime soon."

Concern showed on his face.

"What are you doing here?" As the words left her mouth, she remembered the incident at the front desk and felt guilty for snapping at him. "I didn't have time to call the credit card company today, but—"

"I came here for two reasons, and none of them have to do with what happened at the front desk last night," he said, interrupting her. "I'm not even thinking about our incidental policy. I know you're good for it."

Claudia sighed in relief and smiled her thanks. At least she didn't have to worry about being tossed out of the suite.

"I'm here on official resort business, but first I need to apologize."

"For?" she asked, hoping he'd fill in the blanks.

"I feel horrible for standing you up this morning."

Well, I'll be. Shocked by this unexpected turn of events, she leaned against the couch to steady her tired, wobbly legs. Santiago had stood her up? It shouldn't have mattered, but it did. Claudia didn't know why she was surprised by his confession. This was the story of her life. Men hurt her, apologized, then did it again for good measure. If she had a quarter for every time a man had disappointed her, she could pay off her mortgage and finally take Max on that Mediterranean cruise she'd been dreaming of for years.

"I didn't hear my alarm go off, and by the time I woke up it was nine-thirty, and you had already left." His expression was solemn, but his voice was strong. He strode toward her like a man on a mission, like a man who could crush her will-power *and* her heart.

Claudia backed into the floor lamp and winced when her foot struck the base. There was nowhere to run, nowhere to hide. Shaking her head, she cleaned her sweaty palms along the side of her shorts. Who was she kidding? She could hardly walk, let alone run. And where was she going to go? Into the doorless en suite bathroom? The thought of fleeing to the bathroom made Claudia laugh inside.

"This is for you," Santiago said, offering the flower-print bag he'd had concealed behind his back. "I picked it up in the resort gift shop. It's our most popular seller, and one of my all-time favorites, too."

The scent of cocoa was so thick in the air Claudia's mouth watered. Opening the bag, she reached inside and pulled out a ceramic angel cookie jar. It had intricate hand-painted designs along the top of the canister and the word *hope* written throughout. Claudia was ready to dig in, but since Santiago was watching, she curbed her enthusiasm and read the tag attached to the jar. "Shaped in a traditional fleur-de-lis design, each chocolate cookie has been mixed with the finest ingredients and baked with a mother's love." Claudia licked her lips and rubbed a hand over her stomach. "I can hardly wait to try one. I absolutely adore chocolate."

"Most women do."

His smile was sweeter than the scent swirling around the room.

"Few people know this, but chocolate and chili were discovered in Mexico. These cookies are a marriage of both, and people all over the world order our jars."

"Santiago, you have been terribly kind, and saying thank you just doesn't seem enough."

He shook his head, shrugged a shoulder. "I haven't done anything special."

"Yes, you have. You bought me lunch yesterday at the airport lounge in Washington, escorted me to my suite last night, and now you're here with cookies. You're a modern-day Prince Charming!"

"Who needs a louder alarm clock!" Santiago chuckled. "Aside from the scorching heat, how was your hike?"

"Brutal. I hurt like you wouldn't believe."

"I tried to tell you not to go alone, but you wouldn't listen to me."

"What did you expect me to do? You stood me up, remember?" Claudia couldn't resist teasing him. Not when he looked so smug, so confident. It was hard to believe that they'd only met yesterday. She didn't know much about Santiago, but she liked him immensely. "You should feel bad for standing me up," she said, fighting a smile. "If we had gone together, I wouldn't be in so much pain now. I think you owe me a lot more than a jar of cookies."

"You're right. I do." Santiago placed a hand on her forearm, lightly.

Claudia stopped breathing.

His touch prickled her skin and caused goose bumps to erupt across her arms. A sensual wave assaulted her, left her feeling so flustered she couldn't speak. Which was just as well, because all she could think about was kissing him until she was breathless. Deep down, she wanted more. She ached for him, and the luscious smile stretched across his lips made her desire every inch of him.

Guilt attacked Claudia, making her feel dirty and ashamed for ogling his thick, bulging biceps. Surely, she wasn't the only female guest who'd had sinful thoughts about him. He probably hooked up with a lot of women at the resort. But not her.

Ignoring the throbbing between her legs, she withdrew her

hand and folded her arms. Claudia caught a whiff of her shirt and almost fainted. She smelled like she hadn't showered in days, and wondered how Santiago could stand being so close to her. *Time to bring this visit to an end,* she decided, resisting the urge to plug her nose. "Thanks for stopping by," she said, moving toward the door with renewed energy. "I really need to take a shower and get down to work. I'm planning a fantasy ball, and I promised my assistant I'd send my preliminary notes by the end of the day."

"I understand. I actually came over here to discuss a project I thought you might be interested in, but since you've already got your plate full, I'll be on my way."

"What project?"

Santiago waved off her question with his hand. "Forget it. I don't know what I was thinking. I'm sure you wouldn't be interested."

"You won't know unless you ask."

He watched a frown crease her forehead and knew he'd piqued her curiosity. "We're looking for an event coordinator to plan our twenty-fifth anniversary bash, and since that's your area of expertise, I thought you might want the job. But never mind. You're busy."

"I can spare a few minutes now to discuss it."

"I couldn't ask you to do that. I've already taken up enough of your time." Santiago opened the door. "Enjoy the rest of your evening, Señorita Jeffries."

Claudia touched his forearm. "Hold on! I'd like to hear more about the job."

Smiling inwardly, Santiago slowly pivoted back around.

"What exactly does the job entail?" she asked, her eyes wide with interest. There was a note of apprehension in her voice, but also a hint of excitement. "Would I have complete creative control or would I be working with a team?"

"The resort turns twenty-five this year, and we want to throw the biggest celebration ever. We'll be unveiling our new fantasy suites and the wedding chapel at the event as well," he explained. "So, basically we're looking for someone to plan, promote and orchestrate the event."

A smile fell across Claudia's face, lighting her mouth with joy.

"If you take the job, we'll comp your meals, drinks and spa treatments and…" He paused, waited a moment for his words to sink in, then said, "Pay you twenty-five thousand dollars."

Her eyes doubled in size. "Twenty-five thousand dollars?"

"Cash," he tossed out, hoping that would be enough incentive to seal the deal. Paying her off the books was against company protocol, and if his mother ever found out there would be hell to pay, but Claudia was worth the potential ass-kicking.

"I'll need some time to think about it."

"I see." Santiago pulled back the sleeve of his shirt and made his eyes wide. "I have to go or I'll be late for my meeting, and the last thing I want to do is annoy my boss."

"Are you free tonight?" she asked, trailing him out into the hallway. "Maybe you could come back later and we could finish our discussion."

"I'm sorry, but I really don't have time. I need to hire an event planner as soon as possible, and since you're not interested—"

"But I am."

"Good, then let's meet at the outdoor café and finalize the deal over dinner."

Claudia's smile lost its warmth. "It's noisy there, and crowded. Hardly the right place to talk. And we'll probably end up waiting a long time to be served."

"Is there somewhere else you'd prefer to go?"

"No. I'd rather stay here. In my suite."

A grin crowned Santiago's face. This was too good to be true! But as he gave more thought to her suggestion, his excitement waned. Having dinner in her suite wouldn't be special or memorable or exciting. They were in Cabo, a land of destiny and promise, and one of the most romantic places on the earth. Santiago would have loved nothing more than to show Claudia his beloved country. They needed to be out, together, enjoying life. And Santiago knew just where to go. Besides, once they finished planning the celebration bash there would be plenty of time for cozy, intimate dinners. But tonight, they'd talk business.

"Do you have a problem having dinner here?" she asked, a scowl bruising her lips.

"I can't. It's against company policy." Santiago felt his right eye twitch and averted his gaze. Lying made him feel guilty, but if twisting the truth would bring him closer to Claudia, he'd gladly recite a thousand Hail Marys. "Employees are forbidden from dining with guests in their suites, and I want to set the right example for my staff."

Claudia sighed. "Let's just forget it then."

"I know the perfect place we can go. It's quiet, secluded and far away from the crowds."

"I like it already. Should we meet in the lobby at six o'clock?"

Her eyes held him hostage, caressed him as tenderly as a hand along his jaw. Santiago wanted to kiss her until he had nothing left, but gave her a peck on the cheek instead. "Make it seven, and Claudia…"

"Yes?"

"Don't keep me waiting."

Chapter 9

"What's this nonsense about you firing my event coordinator?"

Santiago stared at his mother as if she'd rappelled down from the vaulted ceiling. His eyes wide with shock, he watched her through the dresser mirror, wondering how in the world she'd ended up inside his bedroom. "How did you get inside?"

"I used my master key, of course," she said, waving the white plastic card around like it was a golden ticket. "I have to speak to you, now, and I wasn't about to be put off."

"Next time, I'd appreciate it if you knocked. What if I had female company and—"

"And what? You were watching Telemundo?" Ana barked a laugh. "I love you, son, but you're not exactly smooth when it comes to the ladies. Women love confident men who aren't afraid to take risks, and you're about as safe as they come."

"I'm very assertive. I have to be or I wouldn't be any good at my job."

"That's work. I'm talking about in relationships. Case in point, you dated that adorable cheerleader for months without passing second base. And now she's Miss Cabo."

"Mom, we were in the ninth grade!"

"Yeah, but that didn't stop her from flashing her tatas at every *chico* in the neighborhood, did it?" Ana wore a superior face. "Your father and I raised you to be a gentleman, but that doesn't mean you should be passive, Tiago. Wishy-washy guys never win the girl, but strong, assertive ones always do!"

Santiago squirted aftershave in his palms and rubbed his hands along his jaw. Maybe if his mom saw that he was busy getting dressed, she'd leave.

"Now, back to the celebration bash. I just had a long talk with Ramón and he told me everything." Ana limped into the bedroom and made herself at home on the sofa love seat. "Do you have any idea how hard it was to convince Mrs. Ortega to take the job? It took months of emailing, calling and a lavish five-hundred-dollar gift basket!"

"Mom, are you okay? You're favoring your right side."

"Don't try and change the subject."

Her evasiveness roused his curiosity. Santiago faced her, watched as she struggled to put her feet up on the black leather ottoman. "Did you get hurt during your morning hike?"

"The only thing I want to discuss is why you canned my event planner, so start talking."

Santiago took a moment to organize his thoughts. He'd planned to talk to his mom about the celebration bash tomorrow, but since Ramón had a weakness for running his mouth, he had no choice but to do it now.

"I asked you to review the budget, not to make unauthorized changes. I'm not a whiz at numbers like you, but if I had known you were going to fire people, I would have put in an appearance."

"I didn't want anything to do with the project, but you

begged me to come down here and oversee the renovations while you recuperated from surgery, remember?"

Ana wrung her hands in her lap, intently studying the tips of her French manicure.

"My job is to keep the project on budget, and that's what I intend to do. I know you're a big fan of Mrs. Ortega, but we simply can't afford her. She's too expensive, and in these trying economic times we need to be conservative with our money."

"But she's very well connected in the entertainment industry!" Ana argued, pounding the arm rest. "Thanks to her, an episode of *Destination Weddings* will be filmed in the chapel, and *Eye on Cabo* is doing a feature on us. November is a big month for us, and the anniversary celebration has to be perfect, lavish, unlike anything anyone's ever seen before."

"It will be all that and more. I have complete faith that Ms. Jeffries will deliver."

Ana puckered her lips as if she'd just finished sucking the juice out of a lemon. "Tell me more about this American event planner you hired. How long has she been in the business? Who recommended her? Have you seen a portfolio of her work?"

"Mom, I'll fill you in on the details tomorrow, but right now I have to finish getting dressed," he said, grabbing his watch off the dresser and securing the clasp. "I'll meet you on the patio at noon for the champagne brunch, and we can discuss some of my ideas."

"Where are you going now?"

Santiago slipped on his leather shoes. He knew better than to tell his mother he was going on a date, so he racked his brain for an adequate excuse. If his mom knew he liked Claudia, she'd race back to her suite and start baking a wedding cake, so he didn't want her to know about the Southern beauty with the shy smile. When the time was right, he'd tell his mom all about his new leading lady, but not a moment sooner. "I'm hanging out with the guys tonight."

"The guys? You should be going out on a date!" Ana released a deep, tortured sigh. "I've thought long and hard about your situation, and I still can't figure out why you haven't settled down. Is it that you don't want to get married or that you haven't met the right woman?"

"I don't know." Santiago strode over to the bureau, and after careful consideration, selected a casual white dress shirt. "I honestly haven't given it much thought."

"But you should! You're almost forty!"

Santiago heard the reproach in her tone and chuckled. "That's not old, is it? I thought forty was the new thirty!"

Ana didn't laugh. "I want grandkids, Santiago, and I'm scared that by the time you get your act together I'll be dead and gone. Why can't you just find a nice girl and have babies like everyone else your age?"

"I wish you'd quit watching those stupid reality dating shows, because finding your soul mate is a lot harder than it looks on *Me Encontrarán Una Esposa.*"

"*Find Me A Wife* is a great show, and if you're still single next year I'm going to apply on your behalf," she announced, nodding her head vigorously. "It's time you got married and blessed me with a daughter-in-law I can hang out with and some grandkids to spoil."

Santiago heard the desperation in her voice, felt her loneliness and despair, and said something he knew would make her smile. "I'll see what I can do, Mom."

"That's the spirit!"

Chuckling, he combed his hands through his dark, freshly washed hair. Santiago picked up a bottle of Circa 1840, remembered what Claudia had said about the exorbitantly expensive fragrance, and returned it to the dresser. "How do I look?"

"Like a well-dressed politician!"

"Not this again." Santiago blew out a breath, and combed a hand through his hair. "Mom, I've told you this a hundred times, I have absolutely no interest in politics."

"Not yet, but you will. Imagine, my son, the sixty-eighth president of Mexico. You know, it was always your father's dream that you'd graduate from the finest university and go on to have a long, illustrious political career."

"It's not going to happen, Mom. I'm just not cut out to be in office," he told her, folding his arms across his chest. "I don't have the stomach to lie, and I hate disappointing people."

"You're like me in that regard...so was Marisol." A sad, faraway look filled her eyes, and when she spoke again her voice was a whisper. "Tiago, you deserve to be happy, and it breaks my heart to see you punishing yourself for something that wasn't your fault. Don't let what happened that night stop you from fulfilling your dreams."

"Mom, quit worrying about me. I'm fine. Really." Santiago coughed, but the lump in his throat remained. "The last few years have been tough, but things are starting to get better."

"Eso es una mentira si yo jamás he oído uno!" she scoffed, gripping the armrests and pushing herself up to her feet. "A week after you were discharged from the hospital, you quit graduate school and took off to the States. You have an estate in the priciest neighborhood in Cabo, but you abandoned it for a cramped studio apartment in that bitterly cold city."

"For your information, I happen to like living in Washington."

"Yes, but you *love* Cabo. You'd always planned to raise your family here, but after the accident you tossed all your hopes and dreams aside." Ana touched a hand to his cheek, a loving expression on her face. "It doesn't matter where you run to or how far you go, Tiago. This will always be home, the place where you belong."

"Where is all this coming from? Is this about me returning to manage the resort?"

"No, but it would be nice to have you around. With your father away for weeks at a time on business, I need all the help I can get," she confessed. "Last weekend I promised *Abuelito* I'd come for a visit, but things were so crazy around here I couldn't go."

"I'm sure Granddad understands." Santiago slid a hand around his mother's shoulders and gave her an affectionate squeeze. "He used to be one of the most powerful businessmen in the country. I bet he broke a promise or two in his day."

"I talked to his nurse this afternoon, and she said he has pneumonia. I feel terrible. I should have gone to see him instead of wasting my time wooing Mrs. Ortega."

"Why don't you go down to the village to see him this week? I'm here, and if I have any questions about the renovation project I can always check with Ramón."

Her eyebrows drew together. "You're offering to manage the resort?"

"Stay as long as you want. I can oversee the renovation project and see to it that your desires for the celebration bash are carried out to a T." Santiago retrieved his wallet from the dresser, took out all of the money inside and pressed five crisp hundred-dollar bills into her palm. "Give this to Granddad and tell him I'm looking forward to playing chess when I visit."

"If you're sure you don't mind me going, I'll leave Saturday morning after breakfast."

"Don't worry about a thing, Mom. I can handle it."

His mom pointed a finger at him. "No more unauthorized changes, Tiago." Her voice was stern, and her eyebrows were raised. "I'm serious. And I want to sign off on the event planner's checklist before she orders or books anything. Have I made myself clear?"

Santiago saluted. "Yes ma'am!"

* * *

If I don't time this perfectly it could blow up in my face, Santiago thought, his gaze fixed on his stainless-steel watch. Seconds crawled by. The longer he stood in the foyer, the less confident he was. What if something went wrong and he blew his chance with Claudia?

Santiago shook off his doubts. He'd planned the perfect date, one that the Southern beauty would never forget, and he had nothing to be worried about.

At precisely seven o'clock, he turned off the lights and cracked open his suite door. The apartment was so quiet, he could hear the distant whir of a helicopter. Private tours around Los Cabos were very popular with tourists, and as he thought about the plans he'd made for tonight, he wondered if Claudia would have enjoyed an hour-long helicopter tour. Probably not. She would have deemed it too expensive, a waste of money. And moreover, she'd want to know how he could afford such a lavish expense.

Santiago heard a door slam. This was it. Showtime. Praying it was Claudia exiting her suite, and not that pushy brunette who'd been chasing him around the resort for days, he stepped out into the hall. He caught sight of Claudia in his peripheral vision, but didn't acknowledge her presence. He wanted to get a good look at her outfit, wanted to see if her toned legs were on display, but kept his head down. No sense looking eager. Women like Claudia—who'd been burned countless times by the opposite sex—were suspicious of everyone with testosterone, and Santiago didn't want to blow the little progress he'd made.

"Santiago, good evening," she greeted. "I was just on my way downstairs to meet you."

At the sight of her, his jaw dropped to the floor. Santiago felt like he was having an asthma attack, and he hoped if he collapsed, Claudia would revive him with those glossy red lips. He'd always been attracted to classy, sophisticated women, and her look was a slam dunk. The multicolored dress accentuated her curves and showed off her slender arms. Rhinestone diamonds sprinkled her gold strappy sandals, and she moved with more grace than the Queen of the Nile. She smelled fruity, like strawberries, and he'd bet her mouth tasted sweet, too.

"There are no words," he said after a long silence, "but *stunning, gorgeous,* and *exquisite* come to mind. Of course, they don't do your beauty justice, but they're a nice start."

Claudia had to remind herself to breathe. *In through the nose, and out through the mouth,* she commanded, trying to withstand the crippling heat of his gaze. *And I thought it was hot outside!* Santiago's eyes were ablaze with lust, a passion so intense she could feel the sensual current radiating off his flesh. Fiddling with the buckle on her tote bag gave Claudia something to do with her hands. It was either play with her purse, or stroke Santiago's bulging bicep, and doing him in the apartment hallway was the *opposite* of keeping a low profile. "Stop, it Santiago. You're embarrassing me."

He wore a concerned face, but a grin was playing on his lips. "Now I understand why you hate being in crowds. It must be exhausting fighting off the opposite sex at every turn."

"I don't know, you tell me. How do *you* deal with female guests propositioning you? Is it a perk of the job or a nuisance?" Claudia giggled when a frown eclipsed his boyish smile. "You cause quite the stir whenever you're poolside."

"I don't know what you're talking about."

"Sure you don't," she teased, continuing down the corridor.

Santiago lengthened his strides to keep up with her and opened the door when they reached the front of the complex. He was sweaty, hot all over, and when their arms touched, an electrifying shudder tore through him. Hornier than a frat boy at a wet T-shirt contest, he fought to control the sexual urges attacking his body. An inferno raged inside him, and the warmth of Claudia's flesh incited his desires. The evening breeze ruffled the hem of her dress, drawing his gaze from her lips to her legs. Legs he wished were wrapped around his waist—

"How was your day? I napped for most of the afternoon, but I managed to catch the tail end of the limbo contest. It looked wild."

The sound of Claudia's voice brought Santiago out of his thoughts.

"I had a lot of paperwork to do, so I never made it poolside, but now that I'm off the clock, I'm ready to party!"

Claudia stopped. "Party? I thought we were going to discuss the celebration bash?"

"We are, but that doesn't mean we can't have a little fun while we talk shop. I love cutting loose after a hard day's work and I bet you do, too."

"My sister is always encouraging me to try new things, but I'm just not that kind of girl. My ideal evening is sitting out on my deck, curled up in my favorite chair with a good book. Max thinks that's boring, but being outside relaxes me."

"Max is your sister?"

Claudia nodded, but didn't offer any other information.

Santiago waited a moment. Claudia was a private person, who didn't trust easily, so he chided himself to proceed with caution. "Do you have other siblings, or is it just the two of you?"

"It's just us, and we're incredibly close. Or at least we used to be."

"There's a new man in her life who's cutting into your sister-sister time, huh?" He analyzed her reaction, saw a frown ruffle her mouth, and knew he'd hit the nail on the head.

"Max eloped three months ago, so we don't see each other

as much as I'd like. And now that she's pregnant, she barely has any time for me."

"Your family is growing in leaps and bounds."

"I know, tell me about it." Claudia paused, then continued in a softer voice. "My brother-in-law is one of the nicest guys I've ever met, but he's just too…lovey-dovey. I don't know how Max can stand it. He's always kissing her, or whispering in her ear and rubbing her neck."

"He must be Mexican!" Santiago chuckled. "I'm joking, but Latino men are very passionate. They *invented* public displays of affection, and don't see anything wrong with kissing their woman when the mood strikes. Not even during Sunday Mass!"

Claudia wrinkled her nose. "That's too much affection for my liking."

"How do you know unless you've experienced it first-hand?"

"Because I'm hardly the kind of woman men go wild for."

That's a lie if I've ever heard one.

"I'm not sexy or provocative…"

The erection burning a hole through my zipper says otherwise. Santiago wanted to touch her, wanted to prove her wrong, but he didn't want to risk scaring her off again.

"I read in my travel guide that the resort hosts a charity golf tournament every year. Is it true that you guys have raised a million dollars to date for AIDS research?"

As they ambled along the cobblestone courtyard path, Santiago pointed out the wedding chapel and the row of fantasy suite condos. Claudia was brimming with ideas for the six rooms and had more questions than Santiago had answers.

"I need to stop at the front desk," Claudia said, once they arrived at the main building. "I contacted MasterCard a few hours ago, and you were right. It was just a computer glitch. They're working to fix the problem, but it could take a few more days."

"I told you there was nothing to worry about."

But there is. Claudia felt terrible for lying to Santiago, but she couldn't tell him the truth. It was too upsetting, too humiliating. Thinking about the heated conversation she'd had with that self-righteous customer service representative made Claudia's blood boil. MasterCard had suspended her credit cards indefinitely, without explanation. Not that she needed one. This was the work of the Securities and Exchange Commission. Had to be. Who else was convinced she was a criminal and bent on ruining her?

"Go ahead. I'll wait for you right here."

A low whistle slipped from between Santiago's lips as he watched Claudia glide across the lobby. She had a beautiful face, but the view from behind was out of this world. He prided himself on being a gentleman, on being in complete control, but whenever he was around Claudia all he could think about was kissing her. And making slow, passionate love. Winning her trust was going to be an uphill battle, and if he pounced on her like a dog in heat, she'd write him off as just another guy trying to get into her skirt.

"Take a picture, man. It'll last longer."

Caught red-handed, Santiago hid his embarrassment with a smile and greeted his longtime friend with a nod. Chaz had been the head chef at his parents' resort for ten years, and after the accident, they had become close friends. But not close enough for Santiago to admit he was feeling Claudia. "I'm just watching to ensure everything runs smoothly around here."

"Sure you are."

Santiago threw up his palms. "What? Why are you staring at me like that?"

"I see the hungry look in your eyes. You're mentally sexin' that brown-skinned beauty at the front desk!" Chaz smoothed a hand over the creases in his apron. "Want me to go over there and get her number for you? I don't mind taking one for the team."

"No, thanks. That's Claudia. The event planner I was telling you about."

"You said she was an intriguing woman, but you never mentioned that she was fine." His tone was thick with accusation. "Now I understand why you rescheduled Sheik Mohammed's birthday party. You shut down Sueños so you could have this Claudia girl all to yourself!"

A grin eased onto Santiago's lips.

"You're rich, good-looking and as sly as a fox. I swear some *chicos* have all the luck."

"Claudia doesn't know who my family is, and I'd appreciate if you didn't say anything."

Chaz put a finger to his mouth. "I won't breathe a word."

"Let's hope you're better at keeping secrets than Ramón." The men chuckled.

"I'm going to go check in on my student chef and grab a bottle of Chianti from the bar, but I should be in Sueños by eight. Quarter after by the latest."

Santiago frowned. "Why do you need Italian wine to make a traditional *Mexican* meal?"

"I like to add a few hits of wine to my picante," he said, using his hands to pour from an invisible bottle. "It gives the salsa more kick."

Santiago saw the devilish smirk in his eye and wondered exactly what his friend was cooking up in the kitchen. "What else is on the menu?"

"It's a surprise, but be prepared to see another side of that sexy, leggy beauty, because my secret sauce tends to put the ladies in a *very* amorous mood." He gave a throaty laugh and clapped Santiago on the shoulder. "See you in an hour, my good man."

The chef departed, leaving Santiago to admire Claudia in peace. Watching her on the sly had become his new favorite pastime, but when she turned and caught him staring, he pretended to admire the statue displayed behind him.

Seconds later, Claudia was back at his side, apologizing profusely. "I'm sorry for making you wait, but I just had to get this mess with the suite straightened out. I was scared that if I didn't have a valid credit card on file you guys would kick me out of my room!"

"I'd never let that happen."

Claudia swallowed. His eyes captured her, refused to let her go, and several seconds passed before she remembered how to use her mouth to form words. "There's only so much you could do as the resort manager, and I didn't want to take advantage of your kindness."

"I love helping people, and if there's anything I can do to make your stay more enjoyable please don't hesitate to ask." He leaned in and rested a hand on her forearm. "I'm available day *and* night, 24/7."

Her heart was racing, beating at warp speed. His blinding white smile made her brain short-circuit, and all she could do was stare.

"Do you do much cooking?"

"Not if I can help it."

"I'm surprised. Southern women have a reputation for being amazing cooks."

"Not me," she admitted, with a soft laugh. "I've burned dinner so many times my aunt has permanently banned me from her kitchen!"

"I'll have to keep a close eye on you then."

Please do, Claudia thought, moistening her lips with her tongue. *Please do.*

Chapter 10

Santiago leaned in, closing the space between them. Claudia felt his hand on her shoulder, and when it slid down her back, desire scorched her. Her body began to tremble, and her temperature soared to a thousand degrees. *All that from a simple caress?* she thought, doing her damndest not to faint. *God help me!*

"Right this way."

He led her through the reception area and turned down a narrow corridor lit by round decorative lights. Off the lobby, tucked discreetly behind a wall of waist-high vases brimming with tropical flowers, was the Sea of Cortez plaza.

"I never knew there were restaurants back here."

"There aren't, just one. Sueños is reserved for our most exclusive guests."

"That hardly seems fair. Shouldn't everyone at the resort enjoy the same services?"

"Yes, in theory, but celebrities and high-powered executives don't like partying with the general public. They can hang out back here without worrying about unauthorized videos of themselves landing on YouTube."

Claudia scoffed and made a disgusted face. "Snobs."

"Or maybe they just want to have a quiet, stress-free vacation."

"Yeah, on somebody else's dime." She saw the confused expression on his face, read the question in his eyes, and knew what he was thinking. "I'm an event planner. I know how celebrities are. They can afford to pay for the best, but figure since they're famous they should have it for free. At least, that's been my experience working with the rich."

"Are you always this harsh?"

A long, cumbersome silence followed.

"No," she began, guilt troubling her conscience. "I'm sick and tired of wealthy people being treated better than everyone else just because they have money. I lived in that world long enough to know that the rich are a selfish, screwed-up bunch."

"But that's not what tonight's about. It's about new beginnings, getting to know each other better and sharing a delicious meal." He smiled. "And maybe a kiss or two."

His voice soothed and caressed her. He was wearing an innocent face, but his eyes conveyed his hunger, his need. Claudia recognized it, because she felt the same throbbing ache between her legs. "I'm sorry for going off on you," she said. "I have a lot on my mind right now, but I promise not to let my personal problems interfere with the celebration bash."

His pupils doubled in size. "A few hours ago you were leery about taking on an outside job, and now you're committing yourself to the project. What happened to change your mind?"

My credit cards were suspended, I have a hundred bucks to my name, and the bloodhounds at the U.S. Securities and Exchange Commission are breathing down my neck. Added to that, her lawyer hadn't returned any of her calls. Did that mean he'd washed his hands of her?

Swallowing hard, she touched her throat and discreetly rubbed the knot of fear wedged inside. "I love the challenge of doing something new, and I've never planned an event of this magnitude before."

Santiago plucked a flower out of the vase, discarded the stem and tucked it behind her left ear. "A rose for a rose." He seemed to be studying her face, feature by feature. His gaze pierced and stroked. She could almost feel his hands caressing her flesh, could almost taste his kiss. "I have a feeling I won't be able to concentrate tonight. You're a living, breathing temptation, impossible to resist."

A smile eased its way onto Claudia's lips. She couldn't remember the last time someone had paid her a compliment, and had never received one from a man as captivating as Santiago Medina. "I'm starting to think you enjoy making me blush."

Santiago drew a finger along her shoulder. "I'm a lover of beautiful things, and you captured my interest from the moment we met. Forgive me for staring at you. I just can't help it."

Tingles danced along Claudia's spine and careened down her legs. To overcome the devastation of his touch, she inched back, out of reach. "It looks like we'll have to go somewhere else." Claudia pointed at the sign in the window. "The restaurant's closed."

"To the general public, yes, but not to us." Santiago opened the door, and swept his hands along an imaginary red carpet. "Welcome to Sueños. The place where fine dining, outstanding service and Latin culture meet."

"You reserved the entire restaurant so we could be alone?"

"I did one better than that. I asked the head chef to give us a private cooking lesson. We're going to make an authentic Mexican meal from scratch."

Claudia waved her hands as if she was fending off a swarm of killer bees. "Please tell me you're joking. I'm a horrible cook, and I have no business being near a stove."

"I'll be right by your side, and I promise not to let anything happen to you."

"What good will your word be when I'm thumbless?"

Santiago threw his head back and rocked with laughter. Claudia was a walking, talking paradox. Shy, but witty. Sexy and demure. Equal parts strength and vulnerability. He had his work cut out for him tonight, but he enjoyed a good challenge. Cooking was a great stress reliever, and he hoped that playing around in the kitchen would help Claudia relax.

"Maybe I should just watch. I started a fire in my aunt's kitchen last year, and…"

Anxious to begin their date and to put an end to her protests, Santiago slipped an arm around her waist and gently urged her through the restaurant doors.

She moved purposefully around the lounge, taking everything in. "The decor is amazing in here," she praised, admiring the Aztec motifs and colorful table linens. "It's the perfect venue for a bachelorette party or a family reunion."

With mosaic windows, magenta walls and a fortune's worth of Mexican-themed oil paintings, Sueños looked more like a museum than a restaurant. Glass jars filled with sangrias sweetened the air, and the scent made Claudia hanker for a tall, cold cocktail. The wine-bottle tower was over six feet tall and slanted like the Leaning Tower of Pisa.

"What can I get you?" Santiago asked from behind the raised, crescent-shaped bar. "I don't know how to make cocktails, but I know how to use a bottle opener!"

Claudia laughed. "If it's not too much trouble I'd love a Shirley Temple."

"One Shirley Temple coming right up."

Still admiring her surroundings, she sat down on one of the oversize wicker chairs in the lounge. Her gaze wandered aimlessly around the room, then settled on Santiago. A jolt of electricity ripped through her. Claudia fought hard against her desire and all thoughts of kissing him senselessly. Santiago had arms like the Incredible Hulk, a body that belonged on the cover of a men's fitness magazine and a grin that made her dripping wet. And he was kind, gracious and sensitive to her feelings. It turned out Ana was right. Santiago Medina *was* one of a kind.

Settling back into her seat, Claudia crossed her legs and glanced outside the front window. A stocky man with aggressive chest hair was chomping on a cigar. He looked greasy, like a human French fry, and he had the nerve to wave a beefy paw at her. Scared he'd come inside to talk, she sprung to her feet and hustled over to the bar.

"Here you go." Santiago rested her glass on a coaster. "I hope you like it."

Smiling her thanks, she slid onto the metallic bar stool. "I wish you could make margaritas, because I'd feel a whole lot better about cooking if I had some alcohol in my system."

"Try not to stress about it. It's going to be fun."

"If you say so. I wasn't kidding about being the world's worst cook."

"I'll be at your side, every step of the way." A smile curved his mouth. "Just think of me as your guardian angel, Saint Santiago."

"Quit teasing me," she said, pointing her straw at him, "and fill me in on the details of the celebration bash."

"What do you want to know? Ask away."

"You can start by telling me what happened to the other event planner."

His eyebrows slanted in a frown. "Have you been talking to Ramón?"

"Who's Ramón?"

"Never mind. What makes you think there was someone else?"

"Because you take your job very seriously, and you'd never leave something this important to the last minute. That leads me to believe you either fired your previous event planner, or she quit. So, which one is it?"

"There's no fooling you, is there? Sexy *and* perceptive. I like."

Claudia's whole body—from the top of her head to the tip of her toes—was inflamed with desire, a passion so fierce tremors tickled her hot flesh. "The other event planner..." she prompted, hoping he'd fill in the blanks.

"It's a long, boring story, so I'll give you the CliffsNotes version." Santiago told Claudia everything. About the resort upgrades, his desire to keep the project on budget and Ms. Ortega's exorbitant fee. "I don't mind paying for a job well done, but my suspicion is that she's taking advantage of the owners. I could be wrong, but that's my gut feeling."

"Her fee is high, but not outrageous. Top planners often charge that much."

"But you don't."

"I charge according to the nature of the event, not according to my client's net worth."

"How long will you be in Cabo? I'd hate for you to start planning the celebration bash, then leave midway through the project."

"You don't have to worry about that. I always finish what I start."

"Is that just in business, or in your personal life as well?"

His gaze held her still. Every time their eyes met butterflies gathered in her stomach and she broke into a sweat. "Is there a good selection of specialty stores in Cabo or do I have to travel to Mexico City to purchase what I need?" she asked, determined not to buckle under the weight of her desire. Nailing out the details of the job—not making googly eyes at Santiago—was priority number one. "I have a few ideas in mind, but I have to see what's available first before I decide on a theme."

"You'll find everything you need right here in Cabo," he said, leaning in toward her. "I'm glad that you're taking the job."

"How can I pass up such a lucrative offer? With the holidays just around the corner, that extra money is going to come in real handy."

"I'll pay you half of the money tomorrow, and the balance the day of the party."

Claudia took a sip of her drink. Something Santiago said earlier came back to her. Her only hope of emerging unscathed from William's fraud case was by being honest, so she said, "That's fine, Santiago, but I want things to be done by the book, so no cash payments."

"You're a woman of incredible integrity," he praised, his tone filled with surprise and awe. "Even accountants aren't *that* honest!"

Claudia brought a hand to her mouth to stifle her giggles, but one broke free.

"Seriously though, I'm looking forward to picking your brain about the most effective ways to promote the fantasy suites and our new wedding packages."

"Sure, count me in. Destination weddings are all the rage these days, and if you can find a way to tap into that market the resort will grow in leaps and bounds." Claudia took a sip of her drink. "Is there a vacant office I can use to work?"

"It's real busy around here with the renovations and the constant influx of arriving and departing guests," he explained, "but I'll see what I can do. Tomorrow's my day off, but I'll have the assistant manager look into it."

"Thanks, Santiago. I can hardly wait to get started."

"The next few weeks will consist of long days and even longer nights. Are you sure you're ready for this?"

His stare was bold, as provocative as the hand he'd rested

precariously on her thigh. The anticipation of his kiss was unbearable. And waiting to taste the sweetness of his lips made Claudia feel hot, feverish, like she'd just stepped out of a pressure cooker.

"I can handle it," she said in a confident tone of voice. "I only have one job on the go right now, and once I tie up a couple of loose ends I'm all yours."

"That's music to my ears."

"I know the renovations in the grand ballroom won't be finished for a few more days, but I'd love to take a quick look around if at all possible."

He gave a nod of assent. "What about first thing in the morning?"

"Works for me."

"I'm going to grab some more water. Would you like me to refresh your drink?"

"No thanks. I'm good."

Santiago returned to the bar and ducked underneath the limestone counter. Seconds later, soft music flooded the restaurant. Claudia instantly recognized the low, melancholy voice. It was Lucho Gatica, one of the greatest Latin singers of all time. The heartfelt ballad reminded her of happier times and took her back to her college days, when she was young and free and didn't have a care in the world. Singing along, she swayed her body to the rhythm of the timbales. "I haven't heard this song in years."

"I'm surprised you even know who Lucho Gatica is," he confessed, resting his arms on the counter. "Few people outside of the Latin community do."

"In college, I roomed with a Colombian girl, and we used to listen to her Spanish tapes on my cheap stereo for hours. Valencia was like a big sister to me. She helped me study, made the most incredible gazpacho and taught me how to say dirty words in Spanish!"

Santiago chuckled. "Are you still friends?"

"No, unfortunately, we lost touch when she returned home, but I think about her all the time. I bet she's a busy wife and mother with a bunch of kids."

"Or a happily single career woman like you."

"This is not the life I wanted." Claudia winced. Wishing she could cram the words back into her mouth, she furiously stirred her drink with her straw. "I love what I do, but growing up I always dreamed of being a stay-at-home mom. I was going to have two girls and a boy."

Santiago stared into her eyes, saw the flicker of regret that darkened her face. "You're still young. You could have ten kids if that's really what you want!" he joked. "You have plenty of time to shape your destiny and—"

"I've been knocked down so many times that it's getting harder and harder to get back up."

"I know how you feel," he confessed, slowly nodding his head. "Setbacks are a part of life, a part of being human, and I've had more than my fair share. If it wasn't for my faith, my family, and a really great therapist I wouldn't be here today!"

Claudia cranked her head to the right and studied him intently for several long seconds. "Just how old *are* you?"

"Guess."

"When you first approached me at the airport lounge, I thought you were my age, but now I'm not so sure." As stressed out as a game show contestant in the dreaded lightning round, she gnawed on the inside of her cheek. Santiago exuded the essence of Latin culture—the passion, the vibrancy, the warmth—which lead her to believe he was older than he looked. Following her hunch, she said confidently, "You're thirty."

"Tack on ten more years."

Claudia gripped the side of her stool to keep from sliding off. Sitting there, with her mouth open, she stared wide-eyed at Santiago. "No way," she stammered, shaking her head. "You're lying."

"It's true. I was born on a sweltering August day in nineteen seventy-two."

"But you look so young…younger than me, even!"

Santiago chuckled.

"I can't believe you're forty," she said, still trying to wrap her brain around their ten-year age difference. "What's your secret?"

"You mean aside from having good genes?" Smiling good-naturedly, he shrugged a muscled shoulder. "I live a healthy lifestyle, I don't stress out about things I don't have control over and being with you makes me feel like I'm on top of the world."

Claudia faked a scowl. "I bet you say that to all the girls."

"No, just you."

Silence fell between them as the song playing reached its crescendo. His gaze gripped her, and Claudia knew if she didn't do something fast they were going to end up crossing the line. Santiago must have had the same thought, because he wiped down the counter and walked around the bar. "The resort chef should be here any minute," he told her. "What do you say we head into the kitchen and get washed up?"

"You go ahead. I'm going to finish my drink."

"You're stalling." Santiago pointed at the sip left in her glass. "If you don't join me in five minutes I'm coming to get you."

That's one threat I hope you make good on. Claudia inhaled his scent, felt herself getting drunk off of his smoldering gaze and disarming grin. She had a serious weak spot for the tall, dark and sexy resort manager, one that crippled her every time she was in his presence. He was all man, all muscles, and he had a physique that triggered hot flashes, rapid heartbeat and dry mouth. At least, that was what happened to her when he was around.

"You should see the spread back here," Santiago announced, his voice rich with humor. "There's enough food here to feed the royal family!"

Following the sound of his voice, she strolled through the lounge and into the bright open kitchen. When Claudia saw Santiago's chef's hat and apron she laughed. "'Kiss me I'm Mexican'? You're either hard up for kisses or a player extraordinaire," she teased.

"None of the above. I'm just a guy who enjoys having fun and making you laugh." Santiago offered his cheek and tapped at the designated place. "Plant one right here."

Claudia giggled. It was impossible not to feel good around Santiago. He never failed to make her laugh, always had a word of encouragement and made her forget her problems back home. Claudia stepped forward, lifted her head and pecked his cheek. "Happy now?"

"Thrilled, actually." Puffing out his chest in pride, he picked up the pink chef's hat from off the counter and placed it on her head. "Perfecto! Now you look like a woman ready to do some damage in the kitchen."

Claudia read the block letters splashed across the matching apron. "'The World's Sexiest Cook'? Ha, ha, Santiago. Very funny."

"I'm not trying to be. You're gorgeous."

His smile filled her with warmth and made her body so hot, Claudia feared she'd pass out.

"Allow me." Santiago lowered the apron over her head, then slid behind her to tie the strings. *What an amazing view.* To keep from caressing her shoulders, he stepped back and buried his hands in his pockets. He feared if Chaz didn't arrive soon, he'd fall victim to his desires and ravish Claudia from head to toe. "Are you hungry?"

"Starving."

"Good, because we're preparing a feast tonight guaranteed to set your taste buds on fire." He added, "That's *if* the resort chef ever gets here."

Claudia fingered her earrings. It gave her something to do besides staring at Santiago's mouth. He was leaning against the counter, his legs crossed at the ankles, the picture of cool. She'd never dream of making the first move, but their chemistry was growing stronger by the second and the urge to kiss him was crushing.

"I apologize for the holdup. There was an emergency in the main kitchen."

Claudia glanced over her shoulder and regarded the Latino man marching briskly toward them. He was as tall and as slim as a palm tree, with hazel eyes and long limbs.

"Let's get the show on the road," he announced, rubbing his hands furiously together. "Lobster paella waits for no man!"

Santiago chuckled. "Claudia, this is Chaz Romero, our award-winning chef and host of Mexico's most popular reality cooking show, *So You Think You Can Cook?*"

"It's nice to meet you," she said with a polite nod of her head.

Chaz lifted her hand to his mouth, then paused, his perfectly groomed eyebrows jammed together in a crooked line. "Chaz and Claudia. It has a certain ring to it, don't you think? Rolls off my tongue like whipped butter."

An amused expression filled her face. "I hope you're a patient teacher, because when it comes to cooking I'm hopeless!"

Santiago looked on in horror as Chaz kissed Claudia on both cheeks, then lobbed an arm around her waist as if she was an old college girlfriend.

"I can perform miracles in the kitchen *and* another room as well." Chaz grinned like a used car salesman. "By the time I'm finished with you, you'll be applying for Rachel Ray's job!"

Chapter 11

An hour later, the trio was hard at work—chopping, mixing, sautéing—but Santiago was boiling mad. Chaz was monopolizing the conversation, and his nonstop chatter made it impossible for him to get a word in. It wasn't all bad, though. Thanks to Chaz, he'd learned some important information about Claudia. She'd been raised in Virginia, was the first person in her family to graduate from college and used to be the lead soloist in her church choir.

"I bet you sing like an angel," Chaz praised. "You certainly look like one."

Santiago ordered himself to relax, to keep his cool, but his frustration was snowballing into something fierce. He wanted to punch Chaz, but he tried to remind himself that Chaz was his friend and would never intentionally steal his new love interest.

"Sing something for me."

"I can't. That was ages ago. Back when I had more confidence than talent." Claudia licked her lips and cleared her throat. "Is there anything cold to drink?"

Chaz opened the fridge, picked up a juice pitcher and retrieved a glass from the cupboard. "You have to try my Paradise Punch," he said, shoving the drink into her hand. "It's all Jennifer Aniston drinks when she's here, and Kanye West calls it liquid crack!"

Claudia lifted the glass to her mouth and didn't stop drinking until it was empty. "This is the best thing I've ever tasted! Can I have the recipe?"

"Of course," he said, winking at her, "but you have to pay me in kisses."

Santiago flexed his fingers, then clenched them in a ball so tight he'd need pliers to undo them. What was the matter with Chaz? There was no rational explanation for his behavior. None whatsoever. The head chef was one joke away from getting body-slammed.

"The squash enchiladas are done." Chaz placed the casserole dish on the counter and whipped off his oven mitts with dramatic flair. "All it needs now is a touch of adobo and a sprinkle of parmesan. One taste of this, and you'll be in culinary heaven!"

Claudia inhaled, then moaned her approval.

Santiago saw her quick intake of breath, saw the rise and fall of her chest. Her cleavage swelled right before his eyes. His mouth drooped open, wet with an all-consuming desire. *I'm no better than Chaz,* he thought, staring at the outline of her perky breasts.

"Those smell delicious," Claudia gushed. "I can hardly believe I made them."

"Believe it, baby. You're a natural in here." Chaz gave her shoulder an affectionate squeeze. "Let's move on to dessert. I love churros, but they're tough to make. If you don't wrap them just right the filling will ooze out."

Santiago dropped his knife on the cutting board and wiped

his hands on his apron. "I'll help Claudia. I'm a pro at folding churros."

Chaz shook his head, but his gaze remained pinned on Claudia. "Keep chopping the vegetables," he ordered. "Those pieces are still way too big. Mince, my good man, mince!"

"I'll show you mince," Santiago grumbled, chopping the head off the eggplant and hurling it into the garbage. Gritting his teeth in silent rage, he stalked Chaz with his eyes, watching every sneaky move he made. The head chef had a reputation for being touchy-feely, but Santiago had never seen him behave inappropriately and pegged the rumors as idle gossip. Now, he realized they were true. His talk was filled with sexual innuendo, so provocative it would be banned on HBO. But the most shocking thing of all was Claudia's response. She was flirting right back. It was unlike her, and it made Santiago wonder what exactly was in that Paradise Punch.

A cell phone rang, stopped, then started up again.

Claudia took her BlackBerry out of her purse, checked the number and sighed in relief. "I've been waiting for this call all day. Please excuse me."

Chaz nodded with a jerk of his head. "Don't be long," he said in a singsong voice, waving a wooden spoon at her. "We still have two courses to make."

Putting the phone to her ear, Claudia hustled through the lounge and out of sight.

"I hate to see her leave, but I love the rear view," Chaz murmured, wetting his lips. "She's nothing but legs and ass and thighs. A real whiplash chick if I've ever seen one."

Santiago almost tripped over his feet in his haste to reach the stove. "Watch your mouth," he ordered, snatching Chaz up by the shirt collar. "I've had about all I can stand of your lewd jokes and come-ons, so scram. We can finish up dinner by ourselves."

Breaking free, a scowl twisting the corners of his mouth,

Chaz straightened his crooked chef's hat. "I can't leave now. I have to finish the dessert."

"I can handle it. I've been helping my mom make churros since I was a boy."

Chaz stirred the pot of caramel sauce then reduced the heat. "Any chef worth a grain of salt doesn't leave his kitchen in the hands of an amateur, and certainly not in the middle of creating his signature dish. A dessert, might I remind you, that Shakira can't live without."

"Go home." His voice was firm. "It's not a suggestion, Chaz, it's an order. Now get out of here before Claudia returns and starts asking questions."

"I didn't mean any harm, really, I was just trying to make her laugh...you know...help her loosen up so she'd have a good time." Chuckling nervously, he used the tail end of his napkin to clean the sweat skidding down his forehead. "You're not going to fire me for flirting with a pretty guest are you? It was all in good fun, man."

"The next time I hear you being lewd with a guest you're getting your walking papers. I won't let anyone ruin my family's business, and your behavior is bound to bring trouble."

Chaz nodded. "Are you sure you don't want me to stay and finish up?"

"I've never been more sure of anything in my life."

"All right, then, I guess I'll be going." Chaz snatched his jacket off the counter and stuffed his arms inside. "Take the sauce off the stove in ten minutes," he instructed, pointing at the stainless-steel pot. "Use the cast-iron skillet to fry the churros and—"

Santiago broke in. "Like I said, I've got it."

"Right, cool. Guess I'll see you in the morning then."

As Santiago stood in the middle of the kitchen, watching the flirtatious chef depart, he had an epiphany. If he wanted to get closer to Claudia, he had to quit tiptoeing around their attraction and deal with it head on. His mother's words came roaring back to him: *Wishy-washy guys never win the girl, but strong, assertive ones always do!* A lightbulb went off in Santiago's head. He had to up the ante, had to show Claudia how he was feeling, and as Santiago glanced around the room, he knew exactly what he had to do.

"I'm sorry, Ms. Jeffries, but my hands are tied."

"But you're my attorney."

"Exactly, I'm your lawyer, not your fairy godmother!" Sawyer Tibbs chuckled. "I can't snap my fingers and miraculously make things happen. The judge granted the order, and until I can draft an appeal, your accounts will remain frozen. That's just the way it is."

Convinced she'd misheard the stout, husky-voiced attorney she'd hired weeks earlier, she jacked up the volume on her cell phone and pressed it to her ear. "You have to do something before the Securities and Exchange Commission ruins me. For all I know, they're digging around in my business finances as we speak."

"No doubt about it," he promised, his deep, raspy drawl climbing an octave. "The SEC has a reputation for being ruthless, and I won't be surprised if they subpoena your taxes for the last ten years."

Claudia wanted to scream, to kick something with all the anger raging through her, but she refused to lose it in the restaurant corridor. Her gaze fell across the framed, floor-to-ceiling pictures displayed on the red walls. A dancer in traditional Mexican clothes twirled onstage. In another, the same woman picked flowers. The model was featured in all of the images and was beaming in each one. Claudia wished she had something to smile about, but the more she thought about her situation, the more hopeless she felt.

"I don't understand why the SEC is pursuing me. I haven't done anything wrong." Her voice wobbled, cracked with emotion, and it took a moment before Claudia was composed enough to continue. "My only crime was marrying a man I *thought* I knew."

"Don't go gettin' all teary-eyed on me, lil' lady. That won't help matters none. Besides, I specialize in fraud cases. I haven't won any yet this year, but it's only October."

"Things are only going to get worse for me, aren't they?"

Claudia heard Mr. Tibbs sigh. She pictured him behind his oak desk, a frown wedged between his eyebrows, a fleshy hand stroking one of his three chins. He did everything at a slow, leisurely pace, but since he charged five hundred dollars for phone consultations, Claudia nudged him out of his musings. "Do you think I'll be named as a coconspirator in the case? Is that what this is leading up to?"

"Can't say for sure, but I am worried about the recent motions the SEC has filed."

You're *worried? Try being in my shoes*, she thought, massaging her throbbing temples. *I could lose everything in the blink of an eye.*

"Judges rarely grant financial injunctions against family members of the accused, so that means either the SEC presented strong evidence of wrongdoing on your part or William sang like a canary and implicated you."

The floor fell out from under Claudia's feet. To make the corridor stop spinning, she slumped against the wall and drew some air into her lungs. She took slow, deep breaths. One after another. Until the wave of nausea passed.

"Are you sure you've told me everything?"

Claudia gripped her cell phone so tight a sharp pain stabbed her forearm. "What are you implying?" she asked, her teeth clenched, her lips pursed. "You think I plotted with William to steal from his company, then helped him cover the financial trail?"

"No need to get upset, lil' lady. I'm just trying to get to the bottom of things. Your husband's created quite the mess and—"

"*Ex*-husband," she corrected, wishing she could reach through the phone and smack the plump, condescending attorney upside the head. How many times did she have to remind him that she and William were legally divorced?

"William never mentioned where his offshore investments and accounts were?"

"For the final time, no."

"You were only married for a month when William started embezzling from Qwest Capital Investments, which leads many people to believe you hatched the scheme together."

"Anyone who knows me knows that I'm incapable of stealing from anyone."

Mr. Tibbs pressed on. "But he must have told you something."

"Why, because the SEC says so?"

"No, because you were husband and wife, and most couples discuss everything with each other, especially their finances."

"We didn't have a conventional marriage," Claudia said, knowing her confession was sure to raise his thick, fuzzy eyebrows. "William had his life and I had mine, and the only time our lives intertwined was during the holidays."

"That reminds me. Your husb—" He stopped midword and corrected himself. "William's about to make bail. From what my sources tell me he could be out as early as Monday."

"I—I—I thought his bail was set at a million dollars."

"His lawyers argued that it was excessive, and the judge reduced it by half."

"Who'd be stupid enough to help William? He's a flight risk."

"Your husband has a lot of friends," Mr. Tibbs reminded her.

"William's getting out of jail, and my accounts are being frozen. How is that fair?"

"I understand your frustration, Ms. Jeffries, but look on

the bright side. You're free to travel, and you haven't been formally charged." His voice was rich with cheer. "See, lil' lady, things aren't all bad. In my opinion, you're in darn good shape!"

Irked by his easy, breezy, life's-a-bowl-of-cherries disposition, Claudia wondered if it was too late to ditch the Tennessee-bred attorney for someone else. Someone who could stand up to those jerks at the SEC. Disappointed in herself for hiring Mr. Tibbs after their free ten-minute consultation, she made a mental note to shop around for another attorney this week.

"What part of Mexico did you say you were in again?"

"I didn't."

"You shouldn't be keeping things from me, Ms. Jeffries. I'm your lawyer. What if I need to conference with you about something or—"

"Don't call me," she told him, cutting in. "I'll call you."

Feeling emboldened by her thoughts, Claudia clicked off her phone and switched off the ringer. She didn't have time to fret about the fraud case or what her ex-husband might have told the SEC. She had work to do and no time to waste. The resort was paying her handsomely, and planning the celebration bash was sure to increase business. And right now Claudia could use all the clients she could get.

Back in control of herself and her emotions, she strode down the corridor with her head high and her shoulders squared. Humming along with the song playing, she swayed her body in time with the infectious beat. The rhythm of the drums and the heady aromas drifting out of the kitchen lifted her spirits. And it didn't hurt that there was a dreamy guy waiting to have dinner with her. *Mr. Tibbs was right after all,* she decided, smirking. *Life isn't all bad.*

"Perfect timing," Santiago said, as she entered the lounge. "Dinner's ready."

"Great. You can tell me more about your ideas for the anniversary party while we eat."

"I never discuss business after seven—" he pushed up his shirt sleeve and tapped the face of his watch with his index finger "—and it's nine o'clock."

"Duly noted. I won't mention it again!"

"Sounds like music to my ears."

"Where's Chaz?" Claudia glanced around the restaurant, searching for the quirky chef with the thick accent and wandering eyes. "Let me guess. He ran out of fresh seasonal spices and went to pick some from the garden."

"He's quite the character, isn't he?"

"You can say that again. I've never seen anyone so excited about cooking with gingerroot. Chaz claims they're rich in antioxidants, but I think he gets high off the smell!"

Santiago chuckled. "Something came up and our esteemed chef had to leave."

"Is he coming back?"

"Not if he knows what's good for him."

Claudia gave a shaky laugh and rubbed her palms along her apron. She was nervous about being alone with Santiago—terrified, actually. There was something about him that did it for her. Something about him that made her hot, wet, hornier than a sex rehab patient. And when he blessed her with his smile, her head spun faster than the blades on the ceiling fan. The heat from the oven, coupled with his piercing gaze and playful smile, made Claudia's body temperature soar to a thousand degrees. Desire pounded in her ears and rushed through her body faster than the speed of light. *Nothing's going to happen,* she told herself, tearing her eyes away from his chest. *I just wish he didn't look so damn sexy in his chef hat and apron.*

"It's time for us to sample some of this food you made."

"I didn't do it all by myself. You helped."

"All I did was mince the vegetables. That's hardly cooking."

"You're right. I was the star of the class." Claudia tried to keep a straight face, but a grin was tugging at the corner of her lips. "I always knew I had it in me to be a great cook, but I never had an opportunity to showcase my skills."

"Have you been drinking?"

Claudia erupted in laughter. "You're just jealous. Chaz said that *I* was a natural, not you."

He narrowed his eyes, but his smile was broad. "An hour ago you were terrified of being near the stove, and now you think you're the world's best cook. Let *me* be the judge of that."

Santiago took Claudia's hand and led her through the sliding glass door. Persian-style cabanas draped in red silk curtains stood beside lean, soaring palm trees. In awe of the view, Claudia stared out into the horizon, feeling as free as the orange-winged birds soaring in the night sky. "It's beautiful out here—so quiet and peaceful."

"I suspect it's been a while since you had any downtime," he said, stopping in front of the largest cabana, "and thought you'd enjoy relaxing tonight oceanside."

Claudia stepped inside the cabana and appraised the simple but sleek decor. Scented candles warmed the space with soft light, jumbo sofa cushions dressed the couch, and the round glass table was covered with a half-dozen plates of food.

"Let's dig in before the lobster gets cold."

After filling their glasses with Paradise Punch, Santiago planted himself beside Claudia and took her hand in his own. "Do you mind if I bless the food?"

Claudia sat there, tongue-tied, but managed a nod of acquiescence.

Santiago bowed his head and began a blessing.

Bitterness infected her, making her eyes tear with anguish

and her mouth painfully dry. Claudia didn't want to remember the last time she prayed, didn't want to remember the disappointment she felt that night in the hospital when her prayers went ignored. And as she listened to Santiago she wondered if this was all an act. He wouldn't be the first man she'd met masquerading as an angel but with the heart of a devil, and he probably wouldn't be the last.

"Amen."

Claudia blinked, saw Santiago staring at her, and averted her gaze.

"I'm glad we met," he said, giving her hand a light squeeze. "I think you could have been nicer when I introduced myself and offered lunch, but I won't hold it against you."

"I didn't have the energy to make conversation, and I was in a bad mood."

"And how do you feel now?"

Hot and bothered. "This is really nice," she admitted, spooning salsa onto her plate. "I'll probably never cook another meal like this again, but at least I'm not scared of being inside the kitchen."

"I told you there was nothing to worry about." Santiago tasted his food. Flashing a thumbs-up sign, he nodded his head vigorously. "Claudia, you nailed the enchiladas. They're flavorful and spicy, just the way I like them."

"They are good, aren't they? The next time I see Chaz I'm giving him a great big hug."

Santiago gripped his butter knife. "Do you really think that's necessary?"

"Yes. He's more than just a chef, he's a miracle worker!"

Claudia picked up her glass and took a long sip of her drink. The gentle whoosh of the ocean's waves had a calming effect on her. Being outside, surrounded by the stars and lights, made her feel better than she had in weeks and put her in a playful mood. "So tell me, Santiago, what do you like to do besides managing the resort and propositioning women at the Dulles International Airport?"

Santiago chuckled. "Typical guy stuff, I guess. I golf, surf, play cards with my friends. I just started a new project, though, and it's taking up a lot of my free time." A grin played on the corners of his lips, then slid smoothly across his mouth. "I'm trying to make headway with a lovely young Southern woman staying at my resort, but she isn't making it easy."

"Best of luck," Claudia quipped without missing a beat. "But don't let the accent fool you. Southern women are notorious for playing hard to get and don't impress easily."

"Then, I better hit it out of the park tonight, huh?"

"I hope you have an arm like Sammy Sosa!"

Jokes flew back and forth during the course of dinner. Santiago leaned back and stretched his arms along the side of the sofa. It was after midnight, but he was wide awake, alert, ready to drink and talk and laugh with Claudia for hours more.

"That was some dinner," Claudia said, ditching her utensils and patting back a yawn. "Thanks for arranging the cooking lesson, Santiago. I had a blast."

He pointed at her ceramic dessert bowl. "But you haven't tried the churros, and I made them especially for you."

"I can't. I'm scared I'll split the zipper on this dress if I keep eating!"

"That doesn't sound like a bad thing."

"I'm a lot of things, Mr. Medina, but an exhibitionist isn't one of them."

Another tear-producing yawn.

"I better take you home before you fall asleep in your ice cream," he joked, affectionately clasping her hand. "Can you walk on your own or would you like me to carry you?"

"I can walk."

"Are you sure?"

"Yes, but…" amusement lit her eyes and a smirk caressed her lips "…when we return to my suite I need you to tuck me in."

Chapter 12

Santiago laughed off Claudia's request as nothing more than alcohol-induced flirting. Claudia slid toward him on the couch until their legs were touching. Her body was pressed so close to his he could smell the fruity notes in her perfume. To conceal the erection growing in his pants, he rested his hands on his lap. There, now she'd never have to know that his body and his mind were at odds. "I think you've had too much wine."

Claudia wore an innocent smile. "I haven't had anything to drink but fruit punch."

"That's true, but Chaz added some red wine to the punch."

"I still want to tuck you in." Claudia giggled, then cupped a hand over her mouth to conceal the high-pitched sound. "I mean, I still want *you* to tuck *me* in."

Santiago's eyes widened. That wasn't her voice. Her Southern twang had taken on a low, throaty texture, one that set his body ablaze. He tried to look normal, unfazed by her thick, sensuous tone, but the closer Claudia got the harder it was to withstand the heat.

"Our time together doesn't have to end, Santiago."

Santiago grabbed his glass and guzzled down his water.

"Let's have dessert in my suite." Claudia put a finger to her mouth. "Nobody has to know you were in my room after dark. It'll be our little secret."

"I never knew you had such a mischievous streak. What other secrets are you keeping?"

"Come upstairs and find out."

For one action-packed second, he considered taking Claudia up on her offer. He wanted to kiss her, caress her, give in to the passion he'd felt the moment he'd laid eyes on her, but Santiago knew better than to act on his feelings. Not now. Not like this. Claudia was offering herself up as dessert, but he knew her interest in him had nothing to do with their attraction, and everything to do with what she'd drank at dinner. "I'm taking you home."

Her lips flared into a pout. "You're no fun."

"And you're full of surprises. I pegged you as a shy, reserved type, but I was wrong. You have a wicked sense of humor and deliver punch lines better than a seasoned comic!"

"I usually don't talk this much," she confessed with a nervous laugh, "but I feel so comfortable with you. Like I've known you forever. I know that sounds crazy but—"

"It doesn't, Claudia. I feel the same way."

Their gazes locked, moved over each other with deliberate slowness.

"Why is a woman as desirable and captivating as you still on the market?"

"You make it sound like that's a bad thing."

"It is," he said. "You deserve to be loved and cherished every minute of every day."

Claudia melted into the plush, oversize cushions. His gaze felt warm, hot on her face, and it caused tingles to erupt from her ears to her toes. There was a gravity about him, an energy so profound her body purred with need.

"You're everything a man could want in a woman."

Claudia touched her chest. "I am?"

"I wouldn't say it if it wasn't true."

Desire slammed into her, stealing her speech and turning her thoughts into mush. Claudia couldn't wait to get her hands on him, couldn't wait to kiss and caress and stroke his rock-hard physique. Being with Santiago made her forget everything—her past, her problems back home, the SEC investigation. He had a body made for *Playgirl,* was as charismatic as a movie star and was probably a beast between the sheets. *The quiet ones always are,* she thought, giggling to herself. *At least that's what Max says!*

"How long have you been divorced?"

"Why does it matter?"

He shrugged a shoulder. "It doesn't. I'm just curious."

"I'm starting to hate that word."

"Do you still love him?"

"Yeah," she scoffed, rolling her eyes, "about as much as I love paper cuts, rush-hour traffic and black widow spiders."

Santiago let out a deep, rumbling laugh.

"Since you like playing twenty questions, it's your turn in the hot seat," she announced, propping her elbow up on the back of the couch. "Do you have a girlfriend?"

"No, but I'm working on it."

"Sure you are," she quipped, her tone thick with sarcasm. "Guys like you love playing the field, and I bet that you have an old college sweetheart on standby somewhere."

"I didn't date much in college. I was such a troublemaker my graduating class voted me most likely to end up on *Mexico's Most Wanted!*"

Claudia winced. "Ouch. That's brutal."

"Tell me about it."

"I bet you don't have a problem getting dates now," Claudia said, marveling at the smoothness of his skin, the fullness of his lips and his ripped forearms. "I see the way the female guests around here flock to you. You're definitely the most popular guy on staff."

"I don't need a harem, Claudia. Just someone I share a meaningful connection with."

His eyes never left her face.

"Our meeting wasn't by chance or a coincidence. It was fate. A moment orchestrated by a force bigger than ourselves." He spoke with great passion, sharing his feelings freely. "I feel blessed to have met you," he confessed. "Honored, actually."

"You feel honored to know me?" The words felt strange on her tongue and foreign to her ears. "No one's ever said anything like that to me before."

"A woman of your intelligence and beauty should not only be appreciated for her aesthetic qualities, but for the depth of her mind as well."

Sighing inwardly, she fought against the smile tickling the corners of her lips. Santiago was more eloquent than an eighteenth-century poet, and his words were filled with such tender warmth that they resonated in her soul. It was the sweetest thing anyone had ever said to her, and to her surprise, she believed every word. "I don't know what to say."

"Then don't say anything." His eyes smiled, swept over her like the gentle breeze ruffling the curtains. "Call me whenever you need to talk or vent about how unfair life is. I've been there, and I know how important it is to have someone in your corner."

Sparks flew when he clasped her hand.

"Thank you, Santiago. I just might take you up on your offer."

"I hope you do…"

His mouth was less than an inch away—poised, ready, waiting.

Their lips crushed together. Moved hungrily over each other with the same urgency as their roving hands.

The kiss was ferocious.

Explosive.

So devastating she'd need weeks to recover from it.

Claudia didn't know who initiated the kiss, but she suspected she'd lost the battle with her conscience and shamelessly pounced on him. The ecstasy of kissing Santiago—finally, after all this time—was just too much. Desire ripped through her, and her lust for him burned out of control. Claudia was aware of the risks of having sex in a public place, but damn the risks! She hadn't had sex for months, and never with a man whose smile was enough to make her wet.

She was breathing in short, quick puffs, like someone on the verge of collapse, but Claudia would rather faint than end the kiss. Not when Santiago was whispering in her ear, caressing her skin, and using his tongue to kindle her body's fire. Her defenses melted away and flittered out the cabana along with her common sense and proper Southern upbringing.

The kiss was urgent, filled with so much heat Claudia collapsed against his chest. Their tongues met, swirled around each other in a sensuous, erotic dance. She loved what Santiago was doing with his lips, loved how moist and tender they felt against her mouth.

What happened to keeping your distance? To keeping your heart under lock and key?

Her conscience troubled her, reminded her of the pitfalls of indulging in a vacation fling. The sensible thing to do was to leave. But Claudia wasn't feeling sensible; she was feeling sexy and daring and adventurous. Tonight, she was going to fulfill her fantasies, and do all of the naughty, erotic things that respectable Southern girls just didn't do.

"I've been dreaming of kissing you from the moment I saw you enter the luxury lounge," he confessed, using his thumbs to caress her face from her ear to her cheeks. "You're exqui-

site, lovely, as delicate as the petals on a freshly bloomed
rose."

Claudia was lost. Lost in the rapture of his kiss, the perfume of his words and the pleasure of his caress. Overtaken
like a ship in the path of a storm, she felt herself being swept
up in a sensual, sexual whirlwind. His lips teased her, stroked
her, made everything in her messed-up world deliciously
right. Santiago's kiss was the best thing that had ever happened to her, and his mouth was so sweet she felt a giddy rush
of excitement.

Her passion snowballed into something fierce, and the
more Santiago gave, the more she took. Claudia had never
known such pleasure, such hunger. Turned on and excited
about the prospect of making love, she lifted her dress and
slid onto his lap. Straddling him, she stuck a hand inside
his polo shirt and shamelessly stroked his bulging biceps.
She kissed him deeply, intensely, with total abandon. Claudia wanted Santiago, here, now, under the curtain of bright,
twinkling stars, and she was going to have him.

Chest to chest, their lips teasing, their hands stroking,
they moved in sync to the tranquil music of the ocean waves
beyond the cabana walls. Aroused by the feel of his body
so close to hers, she rubbed her hips against his erection.
A flame ignited between her legs, causing her to moan and
groan. Claudia was scared couples strolling along the beach
or teens playing Frisbee would hear them, but that only added
to the excitement.

"The strangest thing happens whenever I'm around you."
He drew his fingers along her neck, then buried them in her
hair. An impish grin was playing on his lips. "My palms
sweat and my heart beats so fast I feel like I'm having a heart
attack!"

"Then, I better take it easy on you tonight, huh?"

Santiago slipped a hand under her dress and cupped her
butt. And when he rubbed his thumb along the front of her

panties she shivered like a surfer lost at sea. He parted her lips, massaging her clit with his fingers. He probed her treasure, stroking her with such agonizing slowness Claudia had to take matters into her own hands. She rocked against him, forcing him deeper inside her tight, slick walls. Savage moans streamed from her mouth, shattering the quiet moonlit night. Her heart was hammering so loud in her chest she couldn't breathe. Santiago alternated between tender strokes and quick, urgent ones. She fondled him through his clothes, used her lips and tongue and mouth to devour him.

Claudia was losing it, on the verge of delirium, but she'd never felt such freedom. Finally, after all these years, she was in control of her pleasure. Free to do whatever she pleased. And Claudia wanted to ride Santiago until she had nothing left.

"Slow down," he cautioned, nuzzling his face against her cheek. "We have all night."

Claudia sped up and gripped his shoulders so hard, Santiago knew he'd wake up in the morning with a bruise. Santiago soaked up the sexy sounds of her moans. Concealing a grin, he sat back and watched the sexy Southern beauty do her thing. Damn, Claudia was hot. She wasn't afraid to take the reins, wasn't afraid to call the shots, and when she clamped her legs around his waist, he almost exploded in his pants. Santiago couldn't believe this was the same woman who'd run away from him in the Dulles International Airport lounge. The event planner was a shy, quiet type, but after dark she was a brazen sex kitten. Claudia talked dirty, grabbed at his package, and did things with her tongue that would make a porn star blush.

Claudia felt flushed, wet, out of breath. He tickled the tip of her tongue with his own, and chuckled when she grabbed a fistful of his thick hair. His mouth seared her, set her flesh on fire. The air smelled sweet, perfumed with the scent of their loving and the hibiscus bordering the nearby garden.

She squeezed her pelvic muscles and rotated her hips until the tingling in her feet shot straight to her core. Blood flowed to her breasts, hardening her nipples.

"What do we have here?"

Light flooded the cabana, hitting Claudia square in the eyes. Her heart did a backflip, then slammed into her rib cage, stealing her breath. Squinting, she held up her palms to shield her face from the intrusive light.

"I'm sorry," a squeaky male voice said. "I didn't know anyone was in here."

Claudia sighed in relief when the stranger put away his light. A teenager with acne-stained cheeks stood at the entrance of the cabana wearing a lopsided grin.

"Who do I have to see to get one of these for the night?"

Lowering her head, she slid off Santiago's lap and turned toward the fire pit. Sitting there, watching the red-hot flame, Claudia wondered how one five-second kiss had led to her shamelessly groping and pawing at Santiago.

Her conscience launched an attack, one that made her feel as guilty as sin.

That was wrong. Stupid. A tsunami-size mistake, Claudia decided, shaking the images of their cabana romp from her mind. *What was I thinking? That was the problem. I wasn't thinking. At least not with my head—*

Santiago's sensuous voice interrupted Claudia's pity party.

"None of the cabanas are available tonight," he explained, calmly addressing the intruder. "Check with the front desk tomorrow, and they'll reserve one for you."

The kid pointed a bony finger. "I know you…"

Claudia stopped breathing. Her mouth filled with fear, which grew so full she couldn't swallow. She glanced around the cabana, searching for a suitable place to hide. *Should I duck behind the cushions or dive under the couch?* Her thoughts were irrational but she'd rather look like a fool in front of Santiago than a liar.

"I can hardly believe it's you!" The teen rushed inside the cabana and clasped Santiago's hand and bowed his head. "I'm your biggest fan ever!"

Stunned, her eyes twice their normal size, she cranked her head to the right. As she listened to the kid address Santiago her confusion grew. His excitement was evident, as real as the powdery white sand between her toes. He was rocking eagerly on his heels, and when he asked Santiago for his autograph, Claudia was convinced he was high on some illicit street drug.

"Wait until I tell my homeboys that you're here. I know your family owns the—"

Santiago coughed then addressed the young man in Spanish. Claudia fanned her face with her hands. His hushed, dreamy tone was the ultimate turn-on. She couldn't be more relaxed if he was giving her a foot massage, and when Santiago stood up and escorted the kid out of the cabana, she longed to be back in his arms. The thought of kissing him again, of sitting on his lap and rubbing her clit against his erection, made her nipples harden.

Scooting forward on the couch, she grabbed a butter knife and inspected her makeup. *I don't look half bad for a woman who just had an orgasm.* There was no physical evidence of what they'd done, but Claudia felt different. His touch made her ache for him, and instead of feeling guilty that they'd been caught in the act, she was disappointed that they hadn't finished what they started.

"We should get out of here. It's almost 2:00 a.m."

"Is everything all right?" she asked, dropping the knife. "That kid sounded out of it."

"He'll be fine." Santiago strode over to the couch. "I better get you back to your suite. You have a long day ahead of you tomorrow, and I want you to get enough rest."

Claudia smirked. *After what we just did on the couch I'm sure sleep will be the last thing on my mind.*

Chapter 13

"Where the hell have you been?"

Claudia choked on her coffee. Stunned by the harshness of Maxine's tone, she lowered her mug and stared at the computer screen. Sunshine bounced off the laptop, weakening the picture quality, but Claudia could still see her sister's narrowed eyes and pinched lips. The muscles in her neck were drawn so tight her veins were popping. Claudia couldn't remember the last time she'd seen Maxine this angry, and couldn't figure out what she'd done to set her off. *If anyone should be mad, it should be me,* Claudia thought, folding her arms. *I've been waiting almost an hour for her to log on to Skype.* "Why are you yelling at me?"

"Because I've been calling you nonstop for the last two weeks, and you haven't returned any of my calls." Her voice rose to dangerous heights, and her face was pinched with sadness. "Royce and I have been worried sick about you."

"I'm sorry."

"You should be," she quipped, folding her arms rigidly

across her chest. "You're not supposed to be stressing me out. I'm pregnant."

"I know, Max, and I didn't mean to upset you. I've just been real busy, and by the time I return to the suite at the end of the day, I'm pooped."

"Of course. Sipping cocktails and sunbathing for hours on end is *so* taxing."

"I wish I had time to hang out by the pool," Claudia confessed, staring longingly out the balcony window and down at the turquoise blue water. "I'm planning the resort's twenty-fifth anniversary bash, and it's more work than I anticipated."

Maxine's eyebrows rose. "But I thought the whole purpose of going to Cabo was to get away from everything, including your demanding nine-to-five."

"The resort manager made me an offer I just couldn't refuse."

"Well, I suggest you scale back on all those long hours because you're starting to look a little worse for wear."

"Thanks," Claudia spat, rolling her eyes to the ceiling. "You're a doll. You always know just what to say to make me feel like a winner."

"I'm not trying to be mean. It's the truth."

Claudia patted back a yawn. "I didn't get much sleep last night."

"You were up fretting about the fraud case, weren't you?"

No, I was thinking about the sexy resort manager with the scrumptious mouth. Since their cooking lesson, they had talked on the phone at least once a day, and despite Santiago's furious schedule he made time to see her every evening. Sometimes they met for drinks, other times they strolled along the beach, and last night it was stargazing in a hammock. At the end of their dates, he often joked about "tucking her in," but after a hug and a chaste kiss on the cheek he went home. Claudia was glad Santiago had enough willpower for the both of them, because every time he touched her she wanted to jump his bones.

"You'll be happy to know that all the media attention surrounding William's indictment has died down," she said, brightening. "These days, all anyone cares about is what outrageous thing Steven Tyler will say next on *American Idol!*"

The sisters shared a laugh.

"How are you doing?"

"Great, aside from a little heartburn and some weird food cravings." Maxine glanced suspiciously over her shoulder, then eased forward in her chair. "Girl, I think I'm addicted to peanut butter and onion sandwiches. I've already had two of them and it's only ten o'clock."

"How's Royce doing? Has anything panned out on the job front yet?"

"No, and I hope he gets a job offer soon, because being unemployed has made him a sourpuss, and his constant griping is driving me up the wall."

"Hang in there, sis. He'll find something."

"Have you talked to Old Man Tibbs?"

Claudia laughed. "Why do you insist on calling my lawyer that?"

"Because he reminds me of that sexist troll who used to live next door to us when we were kids. You know, that leery-eyed old man who called everyone 'lil' suga.'"

More high-pitched laughter.

"Every time I talk to Mr. Tibbs he makes me upset. I think I need to find a new attorney. One who believes in me and listens to what I have to say."

"Ya think? I don't know why you hired Old Man Tibbs in the first place."

"He was the only lawyer in town willing to take my case, and his fees were reasonable."

There was a loud knock on the door.

"Hold on, Max. Room service is here."

"No problem. I'm going to go finish folding the laundry. Talk to you later!"

Claudia leaped to her feet and hustled across the room. She opened the door and almost fainted with excitement when she saw Santiago standing there holding a silver tray and wearing a smile guaranteed to make her melt.

"I have a spicy Santa Fe omelette, two sides of bacon, and bowl of tropical fruit salad for one Claudia Jeffries," he announced, strolling into the suite and setting the tray down on the table. "I know how much you love those breakfast fries, so I added a side to your order."

"I didn't know you helped out in the kitchen. Wow, you do it all around here, don't you?"

"No, actually, I volunteered to bring up your breakfast."

"Why, when you're so busy overseeing the final stages of the renovation project?"

"Because seeing you is the highlight of my day."

Claudia smiled.

"How was your hike?"

"It's not as much fun without my hiking partner, but at least I finished the trail this time. I ran into Chaz on the bottom of the hill and he had me in stitches the whole way back to the resort."

"Really? How nice." After a long, awkward silence he spoke. "I'm going into town this afternoon, and I'm not sure when I'll be back. Actually, that's why I stopped by. I didn't want you to wonder where I was when you came into the office."

"Are you going there on hotel business?" Claudia tried to sound casual, but heard the curiosity in her voice and knew she'd failed miserably.

"No, I'm going to pick up my new passport."

"Planning a trip?"

"As a matter of fact I am," he replied smoothly, inclining his heads toward her. "I'd love to go to Richmond, Virginia, to see one of my sexy lady friends, but she hasn't invited me yet."

"Come anytime," Claudia said, playing along, "except in the winter. It snows!"

"I'd walk ten miles through a blizzard to see you."

A warm glow flowed through her, and a smile lit the corners of her lips.

"What do you have planned today?"

"Not much. I might visit the spa or spend the afternoon reading. Why?"

"I'd love for you to come with me into town, but I know how much you hate crowds, and Paradise Road will be jam-packed," he told her. "Today's market day, and villagers from surrounding areas bring their goods to sell and trade."

"Do a lot of American tourists go to the market?"

"Only a handful. Most travelers prefer the malls and high-end boutiques."

Claudia weighed the pros and cons of going into town. She'd been working around the clock on the anniversary party—booking the entertainment, selecting the silverware, designing the invitations—and needed to get out of the resort before she went mad. Since the chances of being recognized were slim, she decided to take Santiago up on his offer. "If you're sure you don't mind, I'd love to tag along. I want to buy some souvenirs for my family, and check out what the specialty stores have in terms of lighting."

"I'll call for a taxi and meet you out front at noon."

"You're not driving your car?" she asked, frowning.

"I don't have one."

"Is it too much of an expense, or are you trying to be environmentally friendly?"

Santiago chuckled. "The public transportation is so good here I don't need one. I love being outdoors, so I bike, walk or, if I'm really pressed for time, I hop into a cab."

"I couldn't imagine living without my hybrid," Claudia

admitted. "Much like here, everything runs at a snail's pace in my city, and I love the freedom of being able to get up and go." *Especially when pesky reporters are camped outside my home,* she thought, remembering the scene outside of her house the night she fled Richmond.

"I must admit, I do miss that."

Claudia heard something in his tone, and sensed there was a lot more to the story than he'd offered. A question burned on her tongue, but she didn't ask it. Sure, they'd made out in one of the oceanfront cabanas, but she wasn't his girlfriend and she didn't want to pry.

"I'll see you later." He kissed her cheek, then strode through the foyer and out the door.

Claudia stood there, inhaling his light, soothing fragrance. One whiff of his scent relieved her stress and put her in a sexy state of mind. Claudia didn't know when or how it happened, but she'd fallen for the charming resort manager. He was always around, always there, and her desire for him was so strong—

"Who's Santiago?"

Claudia whipped around. Clutching her chest, her heart beating loud and fast, she stared at her sister's image on the laptop screen. "You scared me half to death!" she complained. "Why are you still sitting there? I thought you went to do laundry?"

Max held up her sandwich. "I had to make a snack first. Me and the baby are hungry."

"I have to run, but I'll call you tomorrow."

"Oh, no, you don't. You're not going anywhere until you answer my questions. Now, who's Santiago and how long have you two been doing the nasty?"

Claudia laughed to hide her fear. Her cheeks burned at the memory of his passionate kiss, and she felt herself growing aroused at the thought of his urgent caress. Inhaling sharply, she shook the image from her mind and forced her unruly body into submission. "We're not sleeping together, Max. We're just friends. Actually, more like boss and employee since he was the one who hired me to plan the resort's celebration bash."

"Oh, so he works there?"

Claudia nodded, stared down at the living room floor to avoid her sister's intrusive gaze. "He manages the resort."

"And you like him?"

"Yes… No… Well, not in the way you're thinking," she stuttered and stammered.

Maxine leveled a butter-smeared finger at her. "I didn't get a good look at him, but I heard every sexually charged minute of your conversation. Your voice got all low and husky and for a second I thought you were going to pounce on him!"

Claudia wanted to tell Max about their growing relationship, about how they'd talked and laughed for hours, but worried what her sister would think. Ana was the only person she felt comfortable talking to about her feelings for Santiago. She didn't judge, or make fun of her; she listened and offered thoughtful advice. Knowing she'd regret confiding in Max, Claudia decided to keep her mouth shut. So, instead of pouring out her heart, she told her sister about meeting Santiago at the Dulles International Airport lounge, running into him at the resort and the PG version of their first date.

"He made you cook your own dinner?" She wrinkled her nose and made a face that could scare old ladies and small children. "Ugh! What a cheapskate!"

"It wasn't like that Max. It was fun and romantic and—"

"Tacky," Max concluded, dropping her sandwich on the plate. "I just lost my appetite."

"When did you become such a snob? We grew up in Richmond's worst ghetto, but you act like you were born with a silver spoon in your mouth. You're not a Rockefeller, Max."

"Whatever. Just stay away from this Santiago guy, and

dudes just like him, because the only thing worse than a broke man is a cheap one."

"Don't talk about him like that. He's been nothing but kind and gracious to me."

Maxine's eyes grew wide, and she leaned so far back in her chair Claudia was sure it was going to tip over. "Now everything makes sense," she said, tapping her front teeth with her index finger. "Now I understand why I haven't heard from you all week. You've been too busy hanging out with resort boy to check in with your family."

"I don't have time for this. I have a—" Claudia caught herself just in time.

"A what, Claudia? A date with your Latin lover?" Her voice turned ugly, as sharp as nails. "Where's he taking you? To the local bar for nachos and tequila?"

"Why are you being so mean? You don't know anything about him."

"You're right, I don't. But I know his type. The resort is crawling with good-for-nothing Latin gigolos waiting to pounce on lonely American women like you," she explained, her tone losing some of its sting. "What you need to do is ditch resort boy and head down to the hotel's underground plaza. That's were all the moneyed men are. I'm talking about princes, dignitaries, and filthy stinkin' rich oil tycoons who can afford to buy you anything and take you anywhere."

"I was married to a man like that, remember?"

"You're right. William was a jerk, the absolute worst of the worst, but just because he hurt you doesn't mean you should overlook the rich, prominent men staying at the resort and take up with the help! This Santiago guy works there, for goodness' sake." Her cruel laugh polluted the air. "How much money does he make? Sixty pesos an hour?"

"I don't know, and I don't care. If not for Santiago, I wouldn't have been hired to plan the celebration bash or been given a twelve-thousand-dollar advance."

"But he doesn't even have a car!"

"I have to go."

Before Maxine could respond, Claudia logged off Skype. Fuming, her chest heaving and her hands shaking, she stomped down the hall and into the master bedroom. Claudia couldn't believe her sister's nerve. How dare she insult Santiago! He was an honest, hardworking man who treated everyone—from the bellboy to the housekeeper—with kindness and respect. So what if he didn't earn a six-figure salary or drive an expensive car like her brother-in-law, Royce? It didn't make him any less of a man, and she resented Maxine for implying that it did.

Standing in front of the closet mirror, with her hands on her hips and a furious scowl on her lips, she exhaled the bitterness clogging her lungs and slowed her breathing. The anger drained from her body, and her erratic heartbeat returned to its natural rhythm.

The gardenia-scented breeze ruffled the curtains, and caused her gaze to drift to the balcony. A stately yacht glided peacefully toward the bustling harbor. The view was unbeatable, unlike anything Claudia had ever seen. It was in that quiet moment, with the hummingbirds crooning the season's song, that Claudia had a revelation: she cared deeply about Santiago. And not because he was insanely gorgeous or because he had a fit, hard body she imagined doing all sorts of naughty, X-rated things with, either. He made her feel safe, cared for, and he treated her as if she was the most important person in his life. Claudia didn't care what anyone thought about them spending time together—not even Max. She liked Santiago and wanted to spend the day with him. Was that so bad?

Claudia didn't know why, but arguing with Max had left her steamed, determined to prove her wrong, but it had also left her feeling...horny? Thoughts of kissing and caressing Santiago all over flooded her mind, made her hands shake so hard she couldn't undo the knot on her pink satin robe. It was time she quit stressing about what was happening back in Richmond and enjoy what was left of her vacation. And Claudia couldn't think of anything she'd like more than a spellbinding night of passion with Santiago Medina.

Screw what Max thought.

That's why, as Claudia slipped on her black satin bra and matching panties, she decided that this would be the night she and Santiago graduated from friends to lovers. It was time. Time to indulge in a sensuous night of passion with the man she desired. And when Claudia sailed out of her suite at noon, she had a grin on her face, and—thanks to the resort mini bar—watermelon-flavored condoms tucked safely inside her purse.

Chapter 14

"Claudia, come out here," Santiago called, knocking on the fitting room door. "I want to see how the dress looks on you, and I'm not leaving until you show me."

Claudia stared at her reflection in the mirror and examined the emerald-green strapless gown from every possible angle. She loved the vibrant color, loved how it made her eyes pop, but the Badgley Mischka creation wasn't her style. The neckline revealed an immodest amount of cleavage, and the material accentuated her many imperfections. No way was she letting Santiago see her. "It's not for me."

"Let me be the judge of that."

"I don't know why I let you talk me into trying on this gown in the first place. It's all wrong for the celebration bash, and it's way out of my price range."

"You need a second opinion."

"I know my body, and this dress is all wrong. It detracts instead of flatters."

"But who better to judge than a man with impeccable taste like me?"

A laugh floated out of Claudia's mouth. She was being silly, making a big deal out of nothing. She'd show Santiago the dress, then take it off. Butterflies were doing the tango in her stomach, but she stepped confidently out of the changing room and walked over to the wall of mirrors. "I told you it wasn't the right look for me."

Santiago didn't speak. His gaze was strong and intense, and his eyes were full of admiration. "Your beauty never fails to amaze me," he confessed, stepping forward. "You're as glamorous and as sexy as any red-carpet star."

Now he sounded like Ana. Her friend was always complimenting her, telling her that she was a "beautiful child of God" and, although she was out of town visiting relatives, she called every morning with a positive, life-affirming quote. Claudia knew she didn't have the right body shape for the gown and pointed out the obvious. "Look at how it bunches up at the sides. This dress was made for someone tall and slender, and I'm—"

"The most stubborn woman I've ever met. Why is it so hard to accept that you're stunning?" A broad grin filled his lips. "You, my love, could be on the top of any man's lust list."

"Sure. I'm right up there with the Angeline Jolies and the Halle Berrys of the world," she quipped, shifting her feet. "I don't think I'm ugly, but I'm certainly not the sexy bombshell you make me out to be."

"You are in my eyes."

Claudia avoided his gaze and looked out into the crowded boutique. Women with perfect hair and tanned bodies perused sleek, clean displays. They were refined, elegant. Everything she wanted to be but wasn't. "No one's ever complimented me the way you do."

"Your ex-husband never told you that you light up every room you enter?"

"He found fault in everything I did, and nothing was ever good enough."

Santiago moved in so close Claudia could feel the contours of his hard chest up against her back. "If this boutique wasn't packed, I'd carry you back into your changing room to show you just what I think of you in this dress. You look *guapa*."

He lowered his head. "And *magnífica*."

He brushed his lips against her mouth. "And *exquisita*."

Claudia tasted desire on his lips, felt it in his touch and in his sweet caress.

"Wow! I've never seen that dress look so good!"

Frowning, Claudia glanced from Santiago to the voluptuous salesclerk standing at the entrance of the fitting room. "Did he pay you to say that?"

The woman laughed easily. "How do you feel in it?"

"Like a little girl playing dress-up." She sighed and rubbed her hands along the side of her dress. "It's too tight around my hips."

"I'll grab you a bigger size. What are you, a six?"

"I wish." Claudia laughed and shook her head. "Don't bother. I was looking for something with a lot less va-va-voom for the celebration bash. Thanks, though."

Ten minutes later, Claudia was standing at the front counter, staring at the items she'd selected while ambling around the Ooh La La Boutique. There were sundresses and purses, sandals and blouses, and several casual outfits for Max.

"Should I go ahead and ring these things up?" the clerk asked, pointing to the pile.

"Oh, God, no. I'm only buying the maternity clothes."

"You're not getting anything for yourself?" Santiago frowned. "But you love those wedge sandals, and you almost fainted when you found that cashmere coat."

"I know, but I didn't come in here to blow my whole advance," she told him, opening her wallet and slipping out some cash. "I don't need a new dress for the celebration bash anyways. I have something at the resort that I can wear. It isn't a Badgley Mischka, but I like it."

Santiago placed an arm around Claudia and moved her away from the cash register.

"Ring everything up and charge it to my account," he announced, handing the wide-eyed clerk a platinum credit card. "And add some of those satin scarves on the display behind you. Claudia loves pink, and she'd look great in any one of them."

Claudia shook her head. "I can't let you pay for those clothes."

"Why, don't you like them?"

"Yes, but that's thousands of dollars' worth of stuff."

"And?" he prompted.

"And you can't afford it any more than I can."

"I'm not a pauper, Claudia. I can afford to buy you nice things."

"You can say that again. This will hardly make a dent in his wallet," the clerk quipped, a sly grin tickling her collagen-enhanced lips. "And besides, you look like a million bucks in that gown. Trust me, señorita. All eyes will be on you at that celebration bash."

"See?" Santiago winked. "I'm not the only one who thinks you're a showstopper!"

Claudia gripped his forearm. "I don't need any of these things, and besides, there's no way we can fit all these bags of clothes into a taxi."

"I know," he conceded, rubbing a hand along her back, "that's why this lovely young associate is going to have everything delivered to Suite 1164 at the Sea of Cortez Resort."

The clerk gave a fervent nod of her head. "Your purchases will be there within the hour."

"I still don't feel comfortable about this."

"You don't have to." Santiago dropped a kiss on her cheek. "This is my way of saying thank you for all the hard work you've been doing. And for bringing me steak sandwiches all those days I was trapped inside the office and couldn't leave for lunch."

"This is wrong. You shouldn't be blowing your hard-earned money on me."

"Just think of it as an early birthday gift."

A giggle floated out of her mouth. "Santiago, my birthday was three months ago."

"Then it's a *very* belated gift indeed!"

The clerk handed Santiago his credit card and the two-page receipt. Her eyes were glued to his face, and she was salivating like a dog with a chicken bone, but she addressed Claudia. "You're a very lucky lady, señorita. Every woman in here wishes she was you, and for good reason too. Santiago Medina is the ultimate catch."

"He is?" Claudia shot him a look. "You are?"

"If anyone's lucky, it's me," he said, wearing a broad smile. "I'm spending the day with the prettiest woman in Cabo, and if we ever get out of here, I'm treating her to lunch."

"Have a great afternoon, you two. And thanks for shopping at Ooh La La Boutique!"

After thanking the clerk, Santiago took Claudia's hand and strode through the sliding-glass doors of the upscale boutique.

Paradise Road bustled with life and energy. Shoppers meandered along cobblestone sidewalks, vendors hawked everything from fresh produce to rugs, and red double-decker buses carrying wide-eyed passengers crawled down the busy street.

The sights and sounds in the air tickled Claudia's senses. It was exciting to be among the mass of people moving between the train station, plaza and open-air market. The activity in the market was intense. Tourists haggled with merchants, diners drank and laughed outside of cheap cafés, and teens whizzed between stores on yellow mopeds. Wooden carts were stacked high with ripe fruit, mountains of *I Love Mexico* key chains, and colorful T-shirts touted the virtues of tequila and salsa music.

A mother of three sat with her kids on a bench eating snow cones. Claudia felt a pang in her heart, an ache that only the love of a child could fill. The woman looked haggard, like she hadn't slept for weeks, and there was a giant stain in the middle of her white sundress, but Claudia would trade places with her in a heartbeat. She wanted to be a mother more than anything, but two years ago William had shattered her hopes and dreams for the future, leaving her with more questions than answers. *Will I ever get pregnant again? Or be able to carry a child to term?*

"What's on your mind? You're walking beside me, but it's obvious that your thoughts are a million miles away." Santiago slipped an arm around her shoulder. "I know what it is. You're thinking about how great it would be to live here. It happens to everyone, and you'd be surprised by the number of tourists who buy property after just one visit."

"That's what happened to my sister and brother-in-law, and now that I've seen the city for myself I understand why." Claudia closed her eyes and soaked up the sun, the fresh air and the scents swirling around her. "I love Richmond, and I've never imagined myself living anywhere else, but there's something so freeing and tranquil about living near the ocean."

"You know, the resort's going to need a full-time event co-ordinator now that the chapel's finished and the destination wedding packages are available."

"I have my own event-planning business back home, remember?"

"You'd still have plenty of time to work on your other projects," he told her. "Just give it some thought. After the celebration bash we'll sit down and discuss it in more detail, okay?"

Claudia nodded, and when Santiago lifted her chin and

pressed his lips against hers, she melted against him. He was a great kisser, the best, a man with enough skill to make millions at a kissing booth. Being in his arms was heaven on earth. The kiss was innocent, but filled with such passion and intensity it roused her desires.

Holding hands, with stars in their eyes and a smile on their lips, they strolled leisurely down Paradise Road. They sampled some of the traditional dishes offered by vendors and paused every few minutes to take pictures. It was impossible not to feel good in Santiago's presence. He greeted everyone with a smile, chatted affably with the merchants and attracted more female attention than a platinum-selling boy band. Looking seriously sexy in his pale blue polo shirt and khaki slacks, Claudia wondered why a man with his looks and personality was still on the market. And when he blessed her with one of his sweet, endearing smiles she felt proud to be on his arm.

"Is there anyone in town you don't know?" Claudia teased, noting the wide-eyed expressions on the faces of the people they passed. "My Spanish is limited, but it's obvious that everyone greatly respects and admires you."

"Not me. My family. My great-great-grandparents grew up in these parts, and their twelve children worked in the surrounding villages."

"That's a lot of hungry mouths to feed. How did they ever manage?"

"They lived off the land, raised cattle, and when their oldest sons went off to the military, they opened their ranch to weary travelers. Word quickly spread, and soon visitors were coming from all over the country to sample my *abuelita*'s cooking, and to hear her off-color stories," he explained, chuckling to himself. "Once all their children were gone, they transformed their home into a bed-and-breakfast. It was the first of its kind in Mexico, and an instant hit."

"So, taking care of others is in your blood."

Santiago inclined his head toward her then slowly nodded. "I never looked at it that way before. That's just how I was brought up. But I guess in some ways you're right."

"Now I understand why you feel compelled to feed me all day long," she teased, a smile overwhelming her mouth. "You can't help yourself!"

"Good. I'm glad you understand. Now let's go get some fried ice cream!"

Claudia groaned and clutched her stomach. "No way. I can't. I've already eaten enough."

"One bite isn't going to kill you," he said, leading her across the street. "Paradiso Creamery is the best ice cream parlor in the city, and their desserts are out of this world."

The line outside of the tiny shop carried down the street, but as they approached, the crowd parted, making a clear path inside. Santiago placed their orders, then found a cozy table beside the windows. While they waited for their desserts to arrive, they discussed the plans Claudia had made for the upcoming celebration bash.

"I saw a copy of the invitations that were delivered to each room, and I think you did a bang-up job on the design," he said, his tone as intense as his gaze, "and I love all the posters you put up in the lobby and around the resort."

"We're going to have folk dancers, local bands and entertainers, face painting and at the end of the night the biggest fireworks show Cabo has ever seen."

"Wow, everything sounds great." Santiago started to tell her about the big media blitz scheduled for next week to promote the event, but changed his mind. Once the interviews were confirmed, and he had a firm date, he'd surprise her with the good news. "I'm shocked by how much you've accomplished in such a short period of time. My assistant manager was worried you wouldn't be able to pull it off, but I told Ramón you were more than just a pretty face."

Claudia returned his smile. "Thanks for the vote of confidence, Santiago."

"How much do you think it will cost?"

"I'm not sure. Maybe I can come by your place tonight to review the budget." She added, "Unless there's a policy against me being in your suite."

"Not that I know of, and besides, you're an employee now. There are no rules."

Claudia licked the dryness from her lips. *Is it just me, or is the room spinning?*

"Have you given any thought to the menu? I don't know if you've noticed, but Mexican people take their food very seriously. Guests might not remember who performed at the bash, but they'll certainly remember whether or not the crab was fresh!"

"I know, that's why creating the menu with Chaz is on the top of my to-do list. We've already met twice this week, and we're meeting again on Saturday afternoon."

A waiter arrived with two ice cream sundaes then sped back to the cash register.

"Is that who you were with last night?" Santiago cleared his throat and all thoughts of killing the flamboyant head chef from his mind. "I called your suite but there was no answer."

"I met Chaz after his shift ended to hammer out the details."

"At ten o'clock? Don't you think that's too late?"

"No, not at all. I do my best work after dark."

Santiago parted his lips and pushed the question on the tip of his tongue out of his mouth. "Is Chaz my stiffest competition or just one of your many admirers?"

At first, Claudia thought Santiago was joking, but when she saw the hard, unyielding set of his jaw she knew that he was serious. *What makes Santiago think that I would ever be interested in a freewheeling playboy like Chaz?* she wondered, mentally scratching her head. The culinary heavyweight was a riot, but he certainly wasn't her Mr. Right. There was only one man who fit that bill, and she was staring into his dreamy, deep brown eyes. "Chaz isn't my type. He's obsessed with money and fame, and I'm not interested in those things in the slightest. If I was going to date someone it would be..."

"Go on," he prompted, leaning forward. "It would be..."

"You." Claudia touched a hand to her mouth. "I can't believe I just said that."

"I'm glad you did. Now I know my feelings aren't one-sided."

His gaze torched her, made her cheeks burn, her mouth dry. Claudia picked up her spoon and scooped ice cream into her mouth. It tasted delicious, but the cold, sweet treat did nothing to cool her sweltering body temperature.

"I know you're dealing with some personal issues right now, and I don't want to add to your stress, but I'd like to see where things go between us."

At the back of her mind, she remembered Maxine's warning: *Stay away from him, Claudia. He's only going to use you and end up breaking your heart.* Claudia shook her head, refusing to entertain the lies her sister had spewed about a man who'd done nothing but help her. Santiago had a certain something she found appealing, and with all the craziness in her life right now, she appreciated his calm nature and boundless optimism. "I'd like that very much."

"Really?" He wore an exaggerated frown. "You're not just saying that because I bought you ice cream, are you?"

"You're an honest, hardworking guy who derives great pleasure from his work, and I think that's admirable. And you've been a perfect gentleman from day one. You don't drink or smoke or curse, and that speaks volumes about your character."

"Claudia, I'm not as great as you think. I've made a lot of mistakes—"

"I can't believe you returned to Cabo without giving your favorite aunt and uncle a call!" a female voice said. "Now get over here, boy, and give us some sugar!"

Chuckling, Santiago pushed himself up from his chair and wrapped his arms around the full-figured woman with the wild, curly hair. "It's great to see you guys."

"Well, aren't you a sight for sore eyes?" the older gentleman said, clapping Santiago on the shoulder. "When did you get back from Washington?"

Claudia sat there, watching Santiago, and wondered why he was so nervous. He was smiling, but his voice was strained and his shoulders were as stiff as a surfboard. She was so busy watching him, she didn't notice the conversation had stopped until Santiago touched her arm and said, "Claudia, this is my aunt Zabrine and my uncle Estevez."

She smiled and shook hands with the couple.

"We're having a few friends over tomorrow to celebrate Estevez's sixtieth birthday," Zabrine said, when the conversation turned to their plans for the weekend, "and if you're not too busy, Tiago, we'd love for you to join us."

"Do you have to keep telling people how old I am? Isn't it bad enough that I have a head full of gray hair?" Estevez gave a hearty chuckle. "Come by, son, and make sure you bring this gorgeous young woman with you."

Claudia averted her gaze and stared so hard at a portrait on the wall her vision blurred.

"Estevez, stop. You're embarrassing her." A sympathetic smile sat on Zabrine's plump, pink lips. "Please forgive my husband. He loses his head every time he's around a beautiful woman, and all those tequila shots he had at lunch certainly didn't help!"

After another round of hugs and kisses, the couple left the ice cream parlor.

"I'd love if you could come with me tomorrow," Santiago

said, once they returned to their seats. "Like my aunt Zabrine said, it's just a small get-together."

Claudia spooned a chunk of ice cream into her mouth. Meeting Santiago's friends and family was a big step, one that Claudia didn't think she was ready for, but she liked what she'd seen of his relatives immensely. "I'll think about it."

Santiago drew his fingertips so seductively over her wrist she shivered.

"And I know *just* what to do to convince you to be my date."

Chapter 15

"Exotic animals at the celebration bash?"

"Why not?" Claudia demanded, raising her brows. "I think it's a great idea."

A grin tickled the corners of his lips and humor glimmered in his eyes. "Of course you do. You think *all* of your ideas are golden!"

Frustrated that he'd vetoed her last three suggestions, but determined to fulfill the vision she had in her mind for the event, Claudia searched for the right words to win him over. They were sitting in the living room of his sparsely decorated suite and there was a wealth of paperwork and junk food on the circular coffee table.

"I can't believe how poorly these guys are playing."

Santiago had one eye on his file folder, and the other on the soccer game playing on the plasma screen TV. Every few seconds he released a groan of despair, and when he surged to his feet, knocking over the bowl of popcorn on his lap and sending kernels flying in the air, Claudia wondered what had happened to the calm, mild-mannered guy she'd come to know and like.

"Are you okay? You look like you're about to blow."

"I'll be fine once Toluca starts playing some defense and quits turning the ball over."

"Back to the entertainment for the celebration bash," she said, clapping her hands to reclaim his attention. "Having exotic animals at the party would be a definite crowd-pleaser. Guests could pet them, hold them and even take pictures."

"Okay, that's it, no more watching *Animal Planet* for you!" Santiago chuckled and shook his head. "I'm sorry, but we just don't have any room for it in the budget."

Claudia was disappointed, but nodded and said, "I understand."

Santiago cleaned up the popcorn, collected their empty dinner plates and strode into the gourmet kitchen. Done in neutral brown tones, the sprawling five-room suite had high ceilings, suede couches and a soaring wall of windows that offered a spectacular ocean view.

"Do you need anything?"

"Some water would be great—"

A phone rang, drowning out the rest of her sentence.

Santiago dug into his pocket and took out his cell phone. "I have to take this call. It's my mom." He grabbed the remote control and lowered the volume on the television. *"Hola, mamá. ¿Cómo esta usted?"*

Claudia could tell by the warmth of his tone that his family meant the world to him. Maybe one day, when her mom, Aubrey, was clean and sober, they'd have the relationship she had always dreamed of. Until then, she had Max and Aunt Hattie and Ana to fill the void. At the thought of the spunky older woman, a smile curled her lips. Claudia could do without Ana's religious talk, but her good humor was infectious and she gave sound advice.

Santiago ended his call and tossed his cell phone on the granite counter.

"Is everything all right?" Claudia rested her pen on her notebook. "You look upset."

"My dad's back from Acapulco."

"And you're not happy about it."

"I wasn't expecting to see him until the celebration bash." A scowl crimped his lips. "We don't get along, and every time we see each other we butt heads."

"Will he be at your uncle's house tomorrow?"

"For sure. My parents wouldn't miss my aunt Zabrine's party for the world." He returned to the living room, placed a glass of water on the lacquered table, then sat down on the floor beside her.

"Have you and your dad always been at odds?"

"Yeah, pretty much. I got in with the wrong crowd as a teen and got arrested several times for underage drinking and drag racing with my friends. My dad was ashamed of me, but I wasn't a bad kid. I wasn't good in school and had no one to talk to, so I acted out."

"It's hard to imagine you ever getting in trouble. You're such a sweet, upstanding guy."

He stroked his jaw and stared absently outside the balcony window. "My father lashes out whenever he drinks, and for as long as I can remember, I've been his favorite target. My mom did the best she could to protect me, but there was only so much she could do."

Claudia opened her mouth, but didn't speak. For several seconds, she struggled with her words, unsure of whether sharing a page of her story was the right thing to do. In the end, her heart won out. "I know how you feel, Santiago. My mother's been an alcoholic my entire life, and after she showed up drunk at one of my client's weddings, I cut off all contact with her. That was five years ago, and I don't know if she's dead or alive."

"It must have been hard growing up without a stable mom."

"I survived. I had my aunt and my sister."

He lowered his head and raked his fingers through his hair.

"Try not to worry." Claudia rested a hand on his back and rubbed gently. He was an angel of a guy, hands down the nicest man she'd ever met, and it killed her to see him in pain. "Everything will be fine, Santiago. I'm sure of it."

"You're right, it will, because I'm not going to the party."

"But you told your aunt and uncle you would. Won't they be upset?"

"They'll get over it." He scratched at his cheek. "My father and I have always been at odds, but things really escalated when I dropped out of college and took up stock car racing. And over the years things have only gotten more volatile between us. I hate the strain our relationship is causing on my mom, and I don't want her to have to play referee."

"Maybe I could go with you to your uncle's party."

Shock wrinkled his facial features. "You?"

"I'm dying to drive along the coast and going out will give me something to do other than stressing about all the things that could go wrong at the celebration bash."

"What about Chaz? I thought you guys were getting together to finalize the menu?"

"I was planning on seeing him earlier in the day, but if you don't want me to come I'll—"

"No." Santiago fed her a smile. His eyes twinkled, lit up like a star. "I told you earlier I'd love for you to be my date, and I meant it."

"Great, and I can wear one of those snazzy new dresses you bought me."

He chuckled, shook his head.

"What's so funny?"

"You think you're smart, don't you?"

Claudia pinched two fingers together. "Just a little."

"You tricked me, and I didn't even see it coming!" he complained, draping an arm over her shoulder and hugging her to his chest. "You should work for the FBI. They could use someone with your clever tactics!"

Her smile morphed from sweet to sultry. "And what do *you* need, Santiago?"

Silence fell between them, and when he finally spoke, his voice was painfully quiet.

"I need a woman in my life I can trust who loves me for me."

His words bewildered her, left her so rattled, so stunned by the intensity of his tone she couldn't speak. Who said anything about love? Claudia thought, dodging his piercing gaze. Santiago was a hopeless romantic, a Prince Charming searching for his one true love, but Claudia wanted no part of it. Love hurt, and she had the emotional scars to prove it.

"I've fallen under your spell, Claudia, and my feelings for you are so strong I can't even put them into words," he confessed. "I've been waiting my entire life to meet a woman like you, and now that I have, I don't intend to ever let you go."

He spoke with such feeling, with such loving tenderness Claudia's eyes watered. *If he knew what the Richmond press was writing about me, he wouldn't be saying these things,* she thought, biting the inside of her cheek. *Keep it together, girl. Keep it together.*

Santiago cupped her chin in his hands. "I don't think I could survive losing another woman I love, so please don't break my heart."

He lowered his head then, pressed his mouth so softly against hers, and she leaned closer to deepen the kiss. It was a sensuous kiss, one that instantly put her in the mood for slow, languorous lovemaking. Santiago glided his hands up, and down, across and over her body, whispering words of admiration in her ears.

An insane rush of pleasure filled her, rendering her weak, powerless, unable to resist his caress. Claudia felt herself losing control, but fought to keep her wits about her. She couldn't do this. Not after his heartfelt confession. Santiago wanted a lifelong commitment, and she wanted a night of passion. But Claudia would rather be sexually frustrated than break his heart. "I don't want this," she lied, abruptly ending the kiss and turning towards the window. "No good can come from this, Santiago. We want different things."

He stroked her inner arm and drew his fingers over her shoulders and along her back.

"I stopped believing in happily-ever-after a long time ago..." Claudia struggled with her words, but pushed past the sexual haze clouding her mind and spoke from her heart. "I care deeply about you, Santiago, and the last thing I want to do is lead you on or end up hurting you when it's all said and done."

"Don't worry about me. I'm a big boy. I know what I'm getting myself into." Santiago pressed his lips against the side of her neck and used his tongue to make soft circles along her collarbone. "Are you sure you want me to take you home?"

A shiver tore through her. *How did he know that was my sweet spot?*

He must have sensed her conflict, must have smelled the perfume of her desire because instead of backing off, he kissed her hard on the lips. Her nipples rose to attention, she felt warm down below, and she was tingling in all the right places. Santiago licked from her ears to her collarbone and back again, and each delicious flick of his tongue caused waves of pleasure to careen down her spine. The tantalizing mixture of sucking and teasing, caressing and stroking, pushed Claudia to the brink. And when he sucked her earlobe into his mouth, she fell over the edge. It was a direct hit. Her eyes rolled into the back of her head, and for some inexplicable reason she felt the urge to cry.

"Stay," he whispered, lowering the straps of her sundress

and pushing the fabric down her hips. "If it were up to me you'd stay here forever, but I'll settle for just one night."

Claudia closed her eyes and inhaled his rich, intoxicating scent. This was the only place she wanted to be, and Santiago was the only man she wanted. His words gave her hope for tomorrow, made her believe he cared about her and would be there when she needed him. Claudia knew she was thinking irrationally, knew all those cocktails she'd had with dinner had gone to her head, but how could she think straight when Santiago was tweaking her nipples?

"Your body is a masterpiece. The most exquisite work of art," he praised, stretching out on top of her. "I'm addicted, Claudia. The more I kiss you the more I want..."

They undressed slowly, as if they had all the time in the world and traded passionate kisses every time they lost another article of clothing. Santiago placed kisses on her shoulders, along the curve of her spine, in and around her navel. When he dipped his tongue into her navel, Claudia felt like she'd been struck by a thousand bolts of electricity. The moans and groans streaming from her lips drowned out the television, creating a sensuous, lovemaking soundtrack.

Claudia hooked her arm around his neck and pulled him close. Being with Santiago made her feel connected, alive, bolder than ever. Gone were her fears and insecurities. She wanted to please and be pleased. Claudia pushed his shirt up over his shoulders, desperate to stroke his hard, chiseled physique. Faint scars marked his flesh, but they didn't detract from his beauty; he still had the sexiest body Claudia had ever seen. She ran her hands up and down his chest, then replaced her fingers with her mouth. Grazing her teeth along Santiago's nipple caused him to groan. She licked it, bit it, twirled her tongue around it, then sucked it hungrily into her mouth.

Santiago grabbed a condom from his back pocket, put it on and positioned himself between her legs. He used his thumb to massage her clit, then rubbed his erection against it. Back and forth, up and down, in and out. Gripping her waist, he lifted her up off the couch, and entered her powerfully with a quick thrust of his hips.

Claudia buried her face into his chest to keep from screaming out. Santiago took his time loving her, giving everything he had and more. He had more moves than a stripper, and worked his hips like a Caribbean dancer.

To keep him in place, Claudia hooked her legs around his waist. He alternated between soft strokes and fast plunges and made circular motions that kissed her G-spot. The man was a beast, taking everything she gave and more. The intensity of their lovemaking, the sheer tenacity of it, stole her breath and made her feel like she was spinning upside down on a carousel.

Santiago's deep, wet kiss sent Claudia into a spiritual realm, the place where euphoria and ecstasy meet. Feeling his tongue against her earlobe, then flicking against her nipple, triggered Claudia's orgasm. Wanting to be in control of her pleasure, and craving deeper penetration, she thrust her hips and grabbed his butt. Claudia tried to stop shaking, tried to stop bucking against him like an out-of-control mare, but her body had a mind of its own.

His slow, languid rhythm quickened, and then he uttered a loud medley of Spanish words and collapsed into the cushions.

Claudia placed his palms on her cheeks, and he lovingly layered his hands on top of hers. "That was amazing…" Pleasure loosened her tongue, and soon her deepest, darkest feelings spilled from her mouth. "It's never…ever…been like that for me before…"

"You're my dream, my destiny, and I'd love to spend the rest of my days and nights loving you."

Chapter 16

"Santiago, what happened?" Claudia asked, trailing her thumb over the long, jagged scar that snaked down his chest. His arms were locked around her in a fierce hold, one that was impossible to escape, but she relished the comfort of his warm embrace. A delicious languor had settled over her, making her feel closer to him than ever before. "I didn't mean to be insensitive. I understand if it's something you don't want to talk about."

"I was in a car accident two years ago."

She felt his shoulders tense, heard him draw and release a deep breath.

"My sister and I were returning from my cousin's wedding when…" His voice trailed off.

"You have a sister?" Claudia frowned. "I had no idea. I thought you were an only child."

"I am…now…Marisol died in the accident."

"Oh, my goodness!" tumbled out of her mouth. It was a

struggle, but she sat up and clasped his hands in her own. "I can't imagine what you've been through."

"It's my fault Marisol isn't here. I shouldn't have been on the road that night… It was the first day of typhoon season, and it was raining so violently I lost control of my truck and slammed into one of the steel lampposts along the highway." His voice cracked, filled with such anguish it pierced her heart. "The paramedics said Marisol died instantly…"

Claudia let him talk. He was unburdening his soul, releasing his hurt and frustration, and she wanted to be there for him, the same way he'd been there for her.

"If I had listened to my mother and stayed at the resort, Marisol would still be alive."

"But you had no way of knowing what was going to happen."

He gritted his teeth, spit out his words. "Tell that to my father. He blames me for the crash, and stopped speaking to me shortly after my sister's funeral."

"Why would he hold it against you? People get in car accidents every day."

"I've won a lot of amateur racing competitions," he explained, with a dismissive shrug of his shoulder, "and even though the accident reconstruction team cleared me of any wrongdoing, my dad is convinced I was driving recklessly and caused the crash."

Claudia remembered the kid who'd stumbled into their cabana, remembered how excited he was to meet Santiago. And he wasn't the only one. Everyone in town had treated him like a celebrity, nodding, waving, greeting him warmly. "I bet you were a pretty good race car driver," she teased, hoping to draw a smile and alleviate the tension in his voice, "and you probably had a ton of female fans."

"I was ranked number one in my division, but after the accident I quit driving. I suffered a herniated disk, and by the end of a grueling physio session all I wanted to do was sleep."

"How long were you in the hospital for?"

"Four months," he said, dropping his gaze to his hands, "and my father never once called or came to see me."

Claudia entwined her fingers with his. "Everyone processes grief differently, Santiago. Your father lost his daughter, and there was no guarantee that his son would survive. He probably couldn't bear to see you hooked up to all those monitors and machines."

"I didn't want to live without Marisol, and every time I saw the disgust in my father's eyes, I wanted to die. The pain of losing my sister was unbearable, and knowing that my dad hated me only increased my grief. Sometimes all I could do was cry."

Sniffling, Claudia wiped at her eyes and fought tears of her own.

"I tried to deaden the pain with alcohol and prescription drugs, just so I wouldn't have to feel or think, but I couldn't escape my grief. I felt guilty whenever something good happened to me, and I sabotaged relationships because I didn't think I deserved to be happy."

His face was tight, pinched with pain and regret.

"You're a kind, wonderful man, Santiago, and if your sister was alive today she'd be very proud of you and what you've accomplished."

"I talk at high schools and share my story with teens, but I don't feel I've done enough, so this year I'm going to establish a memorial fund in Marisol's honor," he told her, raising his chin and smiling bravely. "She was passionate about the arts, and I'd love to raise enough money to send a couple of kids from her old performing arts school to college."

"That's a terrific idea!" Claudia pumped her fist then clapped her hands together. "I've worked on several charity boards, and if you need help getting the ball rolling, just ask."

"Thank you, baby. I just might take you up on your offer."

"I hope you do. I'd love to help."

He raised his head, scanned her face as if seeing her for the first time. "Where have you been my whole life?"

"In Richmond, Virginia," she quipped, leaning forward and kissing his cheek. "And now that you have a new passport you can visit my quaint little hometown any time."

"Maybe I should fly back with you after the celebration bash."

"Great! I'll book two one-way tickets!"

Chuckling, he folded his arms around her, bringing her closer to him, closer to his heart.

"I was convinced that I'd never find true love," he confessed, the truth spilling from his mouth, one unbelievable, heartfelt word at a time, "and then you strode into that airport lounge like an angel from above and set my heart on fire."

"I did?"

He nodded, tightened his grasp. "I don't know what you're struggling with or what's weighing you down, but you're strong enough to overcome any adversity. You have an amazing inner strength that will see you through—"

"You're the strong one, Santiago, not me. I've faced some tough times in my life, but nothing as traumatic as losing my sister, or someone I love dearly."

Claudia exhaled, dragged her teeth over her lips to prevent the truth from spilling out of her mouth. Hearing Santiago's story, of how he'd lost his beloved sister, made Claudia realize how foolish she'd been. For the last three weeks she'd been holed up in her suite like a mob boss in the witness protection program. Instead of ducking and hiding and stressing herself out about the SEC investigation, she should have faced her problems head-on.

It's never too late to make things right. Wasn't that what Ana said the last time they spoke? Claudia was scared of what the fallout would be, but it was time she quit running from her past and took her friend's advice. Tomorrow, she'd get the ball rolling. She'd call Mr. Tibbs, and ask him to arrange a sit-down interview with the detectives investigating her ex-husband's case. Revisiting her past was going to be painful, but having Santiago in her life made Claudia feel invincible, like she could do anything. If she had to pay a fine or refinance her business loan, so be it. At least the truth would be out and her conscience would be clear.

"I've learned a lot from you these last few weeks. You helped me reclaim my voice, and even though I'm scared of what the future holds, I'm ready to face my problems head-on."

"Courage isn't the absence of fear, Claudia, it's the triumph over it."

She smiled, nodded her head. "I like that."

"And I like you."

"Even though I gave you a hard time that afternoon in the airport lounge?"

"I wasn't the only one you dissed. There were enough of us to start a support group!" Santiago chuckled heartedly. "I plan to be in your life for a long time, so you better get used to me being around."

"I love the sound of that," Claudia said, her eyes twinkling with happiness. "I can't wait for you to meet my sister and brother-in-law. Maybe you can come up for the holidays, and spend a week or two with us."

"You know, we could avoid all the craziness of a long-distance relationship by getting married in the resort chapel. It officially opens tomorrow."

Claudia closed her gaping mouth. "But we just met. How can you be thinking of something as serious and life-changing as marriage?"

"Because love has no rules or time lines."

"You sound like my hiking partner. I told Ana all about you, and she's convinced that you're my soul mate."

"Ana?" He stared at her, wide-eyed and openmouthed. "Is

she a petite Mexican woman with unruly hair, and a loud, boisterous laugh that could shatter glass?"

"Yeah, that's her. We've become really close over the last few weeks."

Santiago threw his head back and had a good chuckle.

"What's so funny?"

"Baby, you've been confiding in my mother!"

"Ana's..." Claudia stumbled over her words "...your mom?"

"Yup. Has been for the last forty years." Santiago chuckled some more. "It's all good. I'm sure you didn't say anything Mom hasn't heard before. In case you haven't noticed, she's fun and witty, and she curses more than 50 Cent!"

"That's not it, Santiago. I told her things..." *Personal things that I'm scared she's going to tell you.* Claudia gathered herself, forced air slowly in and out of her mouth. "Why didn't Ana tell me she was your mom?"

"Probably because she values your friendship and didn't want to scare you off. My mom has been really lonely since Marisol died, and with my dad away on business for weeks at a time, she doesn't really have anyone to hang out with."

"Oh, God, I'm so embarrassed," she groaned, burying her face in the sofa cushions. "I told your mom about what we did in the cabana."

"What did you say?"

"That I've been dying to make love to you ever since."

He dropped his gaze to her lips. "Then, why didn't you make the first move?"

"Because a respectable woman never does."

"Initiating sex doesn't make you a freak, Claudia."

"I know," she conceded, smiling sheepishly, "but I was raised in the South, and my aunt used to say, 'The only girls who enjoy sex are those who get paid for it!'"

Santiago stretched out flat on his back. "You're in the driver's seat now, and I want a repeat performance of our *rendevous de cabaña.*"

"I'm still tired from round one, but your lap *does* look inviting…"

"Take it easy on me this time," he said, clutching her hips. "We're going to my uncle's party in a few hours and I don't want to have to explain why I'm limping!"

Chapter 17

Claudia clasped Santiago's hand and hoisted herself out of the green Volkswagen taxi. Careful not to trip on the hem of her pastel pink dress, she tucked her clutch purse under her arm and intertwined her fingers with his. After a scenic drive filled with vast deserts, vivid blue skies and stolen kisses, the last thing Claudia wanted to do was socialize with a bunch of strangers. She'd rather have been back in Santiago's suite, stretched out on the hammock, eating fresh fruit or making love. But since she was the one who'd encouraged him to attend the party, she forced a smile onto her lips and followed him up the steep, cobblestone walkway.

"Wow, look at this place," she gushed, admiring the romantic, architectural design of the white estate perched up on the hill. "This isn't a house. It's a compound!"

Three stories high, with a winding driveway and a fully fenced yard that bordered the immaculate grounds, the sophisticated home reeked of old-world grandeur. Potted vases overflowing with trumpet-shaped flowers stood on either side of the glass door, and their thick, odorous scent carried on the cool November breeze.

"If you don't mind me asking," Claudia said, shielding her eyes from the afternoon sun, "what do your aunt and uncle do for a living?"

"They own a catering company."

"Is your whole family in the hospitality business?"

Santiago chuckled. "Pretty much."

Crickets chirped, and bees buzzed around the coco palms gracing the expansive estate. Shrieks of laughter, merengue music and the pungent scent of chili filled the air, rousing Claudia's hunger. "It sounds like the party's in full swing."

"Normally, I'd go inside and steal some food from the kitchen, but since we're late, we might as well just go around the back."

"Do you think your aunt would mind giving me a tour of the inside of the house?"

"I'd be happy to. They have a soundproof media room you just have to see."

Claudia frowned. "What's so special about that?"

"You can scream my name as loud as you want and no one will hear you." The warm, forest-green color of his dress shirt drew out the golden specks in his eyes when he laughed.

"I'm never going to be able to live that down, am I?"

"I've never received complaints before about the noise coming from *my* room," he joked, draping an arm around her and affectionately squeezing her waist. "From now on, I'm going to have to remember to close the windows when you come over!"

Chuckling at the memory of resort security showing up at Santiago's door, they strode past the lush garden and through the decorative archway. Claudia marveled at the size of the backyard. The circular pool dominated the space, but the lavishly furnished porch was the focal point of the yard. People were everywhere. Socializing at the refreshment tables, tanning on plush, chaise loungers, frolicking in the hot tub.

"Goodness," Claudia said, shaking her head. "If this is what your aunt calls a 'little get-together,' I'd love to see what she considers a party!"

"My uncle used to be the mayor of this region, so they know a lot of people."

"Are your parents here?"

Santiago shook his head. "It's too early. My dad likes to make an entrance, and since this is just a pool party, they probably won't be here for several more hours. I'd be surprised if they arrived before we left."

"Do you think your dad is going to like me?"

"What's not to like?" He kissed the tip of her nose. "You're smart, and intelligent, and ridiculously beautiful."

"You are *so* good for my self-esteem."

His touch was deliberate, meant to arouse her passion, and it was no surprise to Claudia when it did. They'd kissed and played in bed all morning, but her body obviously wasn't satisfied. And if Santiago didn't stop stroking her neck they were definitely going to have to make a trip to that soundproof room. "I know what you're trying to do," she said, as she wiggled out of his arms. "I'm on to you, Santiago, so don't even try it."

"What? I can't give the woman I love an innocent neck massage?"

The expression on his face and his use of the *L*-word gave Claudia pause. Being with Santiago made her feel blissful, happier than she'd ever been. Their love was real, unconditional, everything she'd always hoped to have, but this time around Claudia was going to be smart, sensible. No gunshot wedding for her. They were going to take things slow, enjoy being a couple and plan their future together.

At the bar, they chatted with some of Santiago's cousins, sampled the elaborate spread of finger foods, and posed for pictures in front of the gazebo. With her blessing, Santiago joined the soccer game on the east field, and when he stripped down to his fitted white undershirt, Claudia had to remind herself to breathe. Fanning her face with her hands, she ripped her gaze away from his chest and admired the spectacular mountain view.

Adrift in a space filled with strangers, Claudia searched the backyard for a familiar face. A smile gripped her lips when she spotted Ana standing beside the barbeque grill. Decked out in bright colors from head to toe, she looked as bubbly as ever, and when Claudia sidled up beside her, she threw her hands up in the air and squealed in delight.

"Claudia, it's so great to see you!" she gushed, giving her a fierce bear hug. "You look amazing, and now your energy has a warm, soft glow."

Claudia didn't know what that meant, but her friend was beaming, and that was always a good thing. "Thanks, Ana. Hiking isn't the same without you, but it's an incredible work-out and a great way to relieve stress."

"So, tell me, how are things going with that handsome young resort manager?"

"The game's up, Ana. I know you're Santiago's mom."

Her eyes widened, got so big and bright, they could out-shine the sun. "Don't be angry with me, honey. I wasn't trying to deceive you. I love spending time with you, Claudia, but I knew if I told you I was Santiago's mom, you'd distance your-self from me and I didn't want that."

"I understand, but I still wish you would have told me he was your son."

"We're friends, and I would never repeat anything you told me in confidence to anyone." A smirk rippled across her plump, red lips. "Besides, I wasn't born yesterday. When it comes to the bedroom, I've done it all and then some!"

A giggle burst out of Claudia's mouth, and the faster Ana wiggled her hips to the music playing, the harder she laughed.

Santiago jogged over, his face dripping with sweat and dropped a sloppy, wet kiss on his mother's cheek. "Mom, I hope you're telling Claudia only good things about me."

"What else is there to say?"

The trio walked over to the bar and refreshed their drinks. "I've been looking forward to this moment all day."

Claudia smiled at the silver-haired gentleman with the broad smile on his lips, and the oversize glass tumbler in his hand. His eyes were the lightest shade of brown she had ever seen, his tanned skin was flawless and he carried himself like royalty. It was obvious that Santiago had not only been blessed with his father's looks but also his distinguished mannerisms.

Santiago placed an arm on her waist. "Dad, there's someone special I'd like you to meet," he said, raising his voice above the noise around the backyard. "This gorgeous young woman is my new girlfriend, Claudia Jeffries—"

"—Prescott," he added, a spine-chilling sneer on his mouth. "Cute haircut."

Claudia's body went numb. Panic-stricken, she felt a ball of terror knotting inside her stomach, and her lungs burned as if she'd inhaled a mouthful of volcanic ash. The lump in the back of her throat threatened to choke her, and she prayed for a quick, painless death. Dying would be better than having her secrets exposed in front of the man she loved, but when Claudia saw the rage in Mr. Medina's eyes, she knew he had something much worse in store for her.

"When your mother told me you were dating a lovely young American woman named Claudia Jeffries and that you were bringing her to your uncle's party, I almost fell off my chair."

Saliva filled her mouth. Her palms were cold, clammy, and for a second Claudia feared that she was going to get sick. She felt dozens of eyes on her and knew that they'd attracted the attention of everyone in the backyard. Touching a hand to her chest, as if that would somehow slow her erratic heartbeat, she waited for the humming in her ears to stop so she could gather her thoughts. Claudia swallowed the painful lump in her throat. She was sweating like a runaway bride, and if her knees weren't knocking together so violently she would have hopped the fence.

"I was so anxious to meet you I canceled my appointments for the rest of the day and caught the first flight out of Acapulco." The disgusted expression on his face matched his harsh, acerbic tone. "I mean, it's not every day that a fraud victim gets to confront the monster who bilked him out of hundreds of thousands of dollars, and I wouldn't miss this opportunity for anything in the world."

"Are you drunk?" Santiago tightened his hold around her waist. "Claudia's an event planner, not a financial investor. You have her mixed up with someone else, but I'm not surprised. This is how you act whenever you've had too much to drink."

"If you paid more attention to international news instead of screwing around with this gold digger—" he spat, aiming a finger at her "—you'd know that her husband, William Prescott the Third, was indicted on ten counts of corporate fraud last month."

"You're lying," Santiago said, "and don't you ever disrespect Claudia like that again."

"You don't believe me? Ask her. I'd love to hear what this little crook has to say."

"Jorge!" Ana hissed, grabbing his arm. "Lower your voice. You're making a scene."

"So what!" He threw his hands up in the air, and the liquid in his glass splashed onto the mosaic-tile floor. "She's a con artist and everyone deserves to know!"

Claudia glanced around at the sea of faces, saw the wide eyes, gaping mouths and sunken cheeks. "I'm legally divorced," she managed, finding her voice, and her courage.

"I haven't seen or heard from William since I kicked him out of our house last year."

"You filed for divorce, then skipped town when the authorities were closing in." His smile was anything but friendly, and his skin was a violent shade of red. "How's that for loyalty!"

Claudia willed herself not to cry. His insults stung, but it was the venom in his voice and the heat of his gaze that chilled Claudia to the bone. She'd seen the same, crazed expression on William's face the night he snapped. Only this time, Claudia wasn't going to cower into a corner and absorb the physical and verbal blows. She was fighting back. "I had absolutely nothing to do with what my ex-husband did, and I feel horrible about the pain he's caused."

"No, you don't. You're just as despicable as he is." Anger blazed in Mr. Medina's dark eyes. "My wife might be blind to what you're doing, but my vision is crystal clear. You weaseled your way into my family and sunk your claws into my son because you needed another rich, older man to take care of you."

What is he talking about? Claudia opened her mouth to speak, to defend her name, but her thoughts were so scrambled she couldn't think of a rebuttal.

"You've got it all wrong, Dad. I never told Claudia who I was or—"

"Ever heard of something called the World Wide Web?" he snarled, glaring at his son with contempt. "You don't think she knows that our family is the second-wealthiest in the country? If you believe that then you're even dumber than I thought."

Santiago stole a glance at Claudia. Unshed tears pooled her eyes, and she was shaking so hard her teeth were chattering. Later, when they were in the privacy of his suite, they'd discuss everything—the fraud case, his family background, her quickie divorce—but right now he had to get Claudia far away from his loud, belligerent father. "We're leaving," he announced, turning to his aunt and uncle, who were wearing matching frowns. "Can I use one of your cars to take Claudia back to the resort?"

Estevez nodded. He shoved a hand into his pocket and dropped a set of silver keys into Santiago's outstretched palm. "The Benz is parked along the side of the house."

"You better take her to the Motel 6, because she's no longer welcome at my resort!"

Mr. Medina's shout startled her, made her legs shake so hard she couldn't move. His resort? Claudia frowned. *What an odd thing for him to say.*

Mr. Medina must have read the confusion in her eyes, because he barked a laugh and said, "You didn't think I'd let you continue staying at my hotel, did you? Ha! I expect you and your things out of that suite within the hour. Got that, Mrs. Prescott?"

"You can't kick Claudia out of her suite," Ana said, shaking her head furiously. "She's planning the celebration bash, and doing an amazing job of it, too! We're lucky to have someone with her expertise in charge of the event, Jorge."

"Find someone else. I don't want her anywhere near me or my hotel."

Claudia dropped Santiago's hand. Her inner turmoil was masked by her outer calm, but she was on the verge of an emotional breakdown. "Your family owns the Sea of Cortez Resort?"

"And a dozen other properties in and around Mexico," Mr. Medina added. "But I'm sure you already knew that. I bet you know exactly how much our family's net worth is…"

Claudia's heart collapsed in her chest. She felt like an unsuspecting employee on the hit show *Secret Millionaire,* only everyone was in on the joke except her. Choking back an anguished cry, she spun around and shouldered her way through the crowd. Her vision was blinded by scalding hot tears, but she stumbled through the gate and flagged down a taxi.

"Claudia, wait! I can explain!"

Ana rested a hand on her son's shoulder and steered him toward the botanical garden. "Tiago, let her go." She spoke softly, just loud enough for him to hear. "She's hurt and upset and she needs some time to process what happened."

Santiago's hands were curled into tight fists, and he was breathing like the last man standing after a battle royale. He felt physically drained and emotionally battered, but he knew Claudia was feeling ten times worse. And his father was to blame. "I can't stay here. There's no telling what will happen if I see Dad again—"

"You leave your father to me." Ana's eyes darkened, narrowed, then shrunk into a menacing glare. "I have something *extra* special planned for him when we get home."

Santiago actually felt sorry for his dad. His mom had a violent temper and was known to throw dishes, chairs and anything else in the house that wasn't nailed down when she was angry. But when Santiago remembered the cruel things his father had said to Claudia his sympathy faded. He deserved whatever his mom had planned for him. Santiago only hoped she wouldn't trash his childhood home in the process.

"I have to get back to the resort. I need to make sure that Claudia's okay."

Ana shook her head. "If you go after her now, she'll only push you away. Give it a day or two and then try talking to her. The shock will have worn off, and she'll be more receptive to what you have to say."

Santiago knew his mother was right, but he couldn't shake the sound of Claudia's bitter sobs. The thought of her being mad at him, or leaving the resort to stay at another hotel caused Santiago to break out into a jog. Then a sprint. Running at full speed, he tore out of the backyard, hopped into his uncle's sleek red sports car and sped out of the estate. He was going to see Claudia, and nothing was going to stop him.

Chapter 18

Five seconds.

That's how long Santiago knocked on Claudia's door before using the master key card he'd swiped from the front desk. He hated breaking the rules and didn't believe in invading other people's privacy, but Claudia wasn't answering her phone or his text messages, and he had to make sure she was okay. At least physically.

Santiago pushed open the door. The scent of tropical fruit inundated the air and made him feel like he was strolling through a mango orchard rather than a five-star hotel suite. The boxes of clothes from the Ooh La La Boutique sat on the couch, untouched, and aside from a few dishes in the sink, the suite was spick-and-span. And empty.

Prepared to wait, he sank down onto one of the bar stools at the breakfast counter and pulled out his phone. Still no word from Claudia. He raked his hands through his hair and expelled a deep breath of frustration. He'd checked everywhere. The office, the oceanfront cabanas, the beach. Claudia loved to stroll along the shore, collecting seashells and splashing her legs in the icy-cold water. She could do that for hours—

Santiago lifted his head and glanced around the room in search of the low, fluting sound. It was coming from the balcony, and as he surged to his feet and shot across the living room, he hoped and prayed that he'd find Claudia outside.

He did.

She was curled up on the chaise lounge, swathed in a knitted pink shawl, staring out at the horizon. The sunset painted the heavens a kaleidoscope of pastel colors, but the warm, tranquil image didn't relax him. His mouth was dry, he couldn't think straight and his heart was drumming in his ears. He wasn't going to feel better until he worked things out with Claudia, wasn't going to be able to move forward until they cleared the air.

I found her, but now what? Santiago stood there, listening to her soft cries, unsure of what to do. He wanted to go to her, to take her in his arms, and wipe the tears streaming down her cheeks, but he didn't. His mother's warning came back to him, whirled in his ear like a police siren. He had to go slow, had to ease into the truth about her past, or he'd risk scaring her off.

Santiago opened his mouth to ask Claudia how she was doing, but she spoke over him, and the sound of her thin, pained voice wrung at his heart.

"Why didn't you tell me who you were?"

So much for taking things slow. Santiago coughed, cleared the knot from his throat. "I could ask you the same question, Claudia." He kept his tone warm and his mood light. "Neither of us have been upfront about who we are, but it's never too late to start over."

"I never lied about who I was. You did."

"I knew if I told you I had money you wouldn't give me a fair chance."

"You made that determination after a ten-minute conversation in the airport lounge?"

"Your disdain for the rich was apparent the second we met," he countered. "I didn't want you to lump me in with all the other wealthy, arrogant men who'd mistreated you in the past, so I decided to keep my family background a secret."

"Do you actually live and work at the resort? Or was that a lie too?"

Hating the physical and emotional distance between them, he stepped out onto the balcony and sat down at the end of her chaise lounge chair. Santiago stole a glance at Claudia and felt his heart split in two at the sight of her sad eyes. "After Marisol died, I moved to Washington," he began, folding his hands in his lap. "I've been working there as a business consultant for the last two years. I only returned to Cabo because my mom was having surgery and wanted me to oversee the renovations at the resort."

"I still don't understand why you couldn't have been honest with me."

"My whole life I've questioned whether people like me for who I am or because of who my parents are, and you were the first person I've met in a long time who didn't care about any of that stuff." Santiago thought about his friends and past loves and how every single one of them had disappointed him. "I thought living abroad would give me the anonymity I craved, but it didn't. Strangers are constantly asking me for jobs or loans, and women throw themselves at me because of the dollar signs attached to my last name. You couldn't care less about my family, or what I did for a living, and that made you stand out from the crowd."

"So, everyone in the world knows about the Medina family dynasty except me?" Claudia shook her head and absentmindedly fingered the silver chain around her neck. "If the media ever finds out about this they'll drag my name through the mud—again."

Santiago struggled for the right words. He was absolutely ready to settle down with her, ready to make the ultimate commitment, and he prayed that she was, too. "I don't care what anyone says about us being together. I want to be with you, and I hope what happened tonight isn't going to change anything between us."

A fierce wind swept across the balcony, ruffling the leaves of the potted plants.

"Santiago, you'll always have a special place in my heart..." She cast her eyes away, drew the shawl tightly around her shoulders. "You were there for me when I really needed a friend, and I appreciate everything you've done for me these last few weeks."

"We became more than friends the first time we kissed."

Claudia didn't know what to say, couldn't force her lips to make an objection.

"And for the record, friends don't do what we did in bed last night...or this morning..."

Pressing her eyes shut didn't block out the image of his face buried deep between her legs, or the picture of his naked body moving fluidly over hers, bringing her to the brink again and again. "We had a couple of passionate nights," she said, ignoring the tingling sensation between her legs and her hard, erect nipples. "That's all it was."

Santiago took her hand and ran his thumb across the delicate flesh between her thumb and index finger. "You said you loved me."

"I was caught up in the moment."

"Do you normally tell lovers that you want to spend the rest of your life with them?"

She winced as if in physical pain. "I've never had casual sex before."

"You were intimate with me because it felt right, because

we fit." He whispered the words and moved closer to her on the lounge chair so he could touch the cheeks and lips and mouth he loved so much. "I've never felt this way about anyone before, and I am not going to let you discount my feelings for you because you're scared."

"Santiago, I'm leaving tonight."

His hands dropped to his lap. "Why, because of what happened at the pool party? Don't let what my father said get to you. He's a bully, and I know firsthand how cruel he can be."

"This has nothing to do with your dad, Santiago. It's about me finally doing what's right, what I should have done three weeks ago. I'm meeting with investigators from the Securities and Exchange Commission next Friday, and I have to go home to prepare."

"I'm going with you."

"No." Her voice was firm, as loud as a steel door slammed shut in his face. "This is something I have to do alone. I got myself into this mess, and I'll get myself out."

"But I've dealt with the SEC before. I know how they operate."

"I don't need you or anyone else to save me," she said, folding her arms across her chest. "If I had stood up for myself, instead of letting William dictate what I could and couldn't do, I wouldn't be on the verge of losing my business or everything I've worked so hard for."

"I don't understand how you ended up marrying a man who cared so little about you."

"William was wealthy and ambitious and I was impressed by how well-connected he was. I didn't love him, but I figured in time I would."

"And did you?"

Claudia shook her head.

"Then why did you stay with him all those years?"

"Because I had nowhere else to go," she confessed, her voice tinged with despair. "I got used to the lifestyle and didn't want to give it up, or risk losing my business that he'd invested heavily in."

"So, he was the one who initiated the divorce?"

"No, I did, after he…"

"After what?" he prompted, resting a hand on her lower back. Santiago loved that Claudia was independent and fully capable of taking care of herself, but if they were going to make it as a couple she had to learn to trust him, had to believe that he'd never intentionally hurt her. "Tell me everything, Claudia. Don't hold anything back. I want to know what happened in your past, so we can move forward."

Claudia shook her head, but when she opened her mouth, the truth spilled out. And the more she talked about her dysfunctional marriage, and the heartache and pain her ex put her through, the stronger and clearer her voice got.

"In public, William was a loving, doting husband, but behind closed doors he said cruel and vicious things to me. His insults were as crushing as a physical blow, and for days after one of his verbal assaults I was an emotional wreck. It was hard to believe that a man who attended church faithfully and donated to charity was capable of such abuse, but he was."

Santiago cracked his knuckles, imagined his fist connecting with her ex-husband's eye. "Why didn't you move in with your sister?"

"Because Max has been rescuing me my entire life, and for once I wanted to prove that I could take care of myself."

"So what did you do?"

"I tried to save my marriage." Claudia pushed a breath past her lips. "But the more I tried to please him the more aggressive he became. I couldn't sleep, I started losing weight, and I got so sick that Maxine dragged me to the doctor. I…" She paused, then said in the quietest, softest voice he'd ever heard her use, "I found out I was pregnant a week before Christmas."

Santiago swallowed hard. The wheels in his head were spinning, and his thoughts were racing a hundred miles an hour. Claudia had a child? Why hadn't she said anything before now? He scanned her face, but saw nothing that revealed her true emotions. Waiting for her to continue was nerve-racking, as stressful as playing high-stakes poker, and when she resumed speaking, Santiago found himself hanging on to every word.

"William had been miserable all week and I thought the news would cheer him up, but before I could tell him about the baby, he started in on me about his dinner being cold. He went berserk. Yelling, swearing, calling me a sorry excuse for a wife. He grabbed my shoulders and slammed me so hard into the bedroom wall I blacked out…"

To this day, Claudia still remembered the panic that seized her when she woke up. Her limbs felt heavy, like stone. Monitors beeped, and the air smelled like bleach and despair. Around her, people spoke in hushed tones, but she recognized her sister's voice. Max explained how she'd found her, how long she'd been in the hospital and the painful details of her miscarriage. It was in there, in Room 1264 at the Chippenham Medical Center, that Claudia decided to end her marriage. William was never going to change, but she could. Forty-eight hours after being discharged, she filed for divorce. "I should have left William the first time he put his hands on me. If I had, my baby would be here and I'd be a mother…"

Santiago swallowed hard. The heaviness in his chest spread to his heart, and as he listened to Claudia, the woman he loved more than life itself, talk about the devastating loss of her child, he felt the same crippling sadness he'd experienced at his sister's funeral.

To overcome his feelings of despair, he drew Claudia to his chest. He savored the warmth of her flesh, the sweetness of her scent, and how perfectly she fit in his arms. "You had no way of knowing what he would do," Santiago said, placing tender kisses along her forehead, "just like I had no idea I'd be in a fatal car accident that night after I left my cousin's wedding."

Deep down, Claudia knew he was right, knew that she wasn't to blame for what William did, but her guilt still remained. Santiago whispered in her ear, told her she was strong, and beautiful and worthy of his love. Claudia felt his hands on her shoulders and shivered when his fingertips grazed her neck. She pulled out of his arms, closing the door on her past and her desire. "You should go. I have a 5:00 a.m. flight, and I still haven't packed."

"But the celebration bash is this weekend."

Claudia pushed herself up. Unsteady on her feet, she gripped the back of the lounge chair and slid over to the balcony doors. "Everything has been done. The only thing I have left to do is finalize the menu with Chaz, but I can easily do that from home."

"You promised to see this project through to the end, and I intend to hold you to that. If you leave tomorrow, you won't receive your final payment for the job."

It was a calculated attack, one Claudia never saw coming, and when she composed herself enough to speak it was with righteous anger. "That's not fair. I've been working my butt off for the last three weeks. Waking up early, going to bed late, running around all day making sure things will be perfect for the celebration bash."

Santiago stood his ground. "I'm aware of how tirelessly you've worked, and appreciate everything you've done, but you need to be here on Saturday in case something goes wrong."

"You're trying to get back at me for breaking up with you." Scared she'd end up saying something she'd regret, Claudia stormed inside the suite, and down the hall into the master bedroom.

"This is business," he said, trailing behind her. "It's nothing personal."

"Of course it's personal! You're blackmailing me!"

Her cell phone rang, but Claudia made no move to answer it. She tossed her travel bag on the bed, unzipped it, and started hurling toiletries inside. "I can't believe you'd do this to me," she raged, stomping around the room snatching things off the dresser and end tables. "You're no different than any other wealthy, powerful man. You're a hard-nosed bully."

Santiago looked wounded, as if she'd shot him in the face with a BB gun, but his voice was strong. "I'm not bullying you. I'm simply asking you to honor the deal we made."

"No, you're holding me hostage. Twelve thousand dollars is chump change for someone as rich as you, but that's a lot of money to me, and I'm not leaving here without it."

"So I have a little money in the bank. Big deal," he said with a dismissive shrug of his shoulders. "I'm not living off my family's wealth or dipping into some mysterious trust fund, either. I've worked hard for everything I have, and I've never used my name to get ahead. I don't need to. I'm damn good at what I do." He added, "Just like you."

"Fine," she conceded, throwing in the towel. "I'll stay until after the celebration bash."

"Thank you. I appreciate it."

Claudia searched his eyes to see if the sincerity in his voice was painted on his face. She'd never seen him look so vulnerable, or sound so intense, and when a soft smile touched his lips, she felt a pang of guilt. Comparing Santiago to her ex was a low blow. The two men had nothing in common, and for as long as Claudia lived she'd look back on this month with Santiago as the most magical, romantic time in her life.

"Is my wealth going to be an issue between us? Because if it is, I can donate every penny I have to charity, pack up and move in with you!"

His eyes were alive with laughter, but Claudia could hear

the anxiety in his voice. She felt the tension that remained in the room and knew this conversation was far from over.

"Claudia, I don't care where I rank on the Forbes list, or how many times I'm featured on the news. None of that matters to me. If I lost everything tomorrow, I wouldn't care as long as I have my family and…you." Santiago took the bottle of hair spray out of her hand and tossed it on the bed. He cupped her chin and leaned in so close their noses were touching. "You're everything I could ever want or desire. You're the one, my dream, my destiny, the woman God created specifically for me, and I plan to spend the rest of my life showering you with love."

Words didn't come. Santiago was putting her on. Just sweet-talking her so she would stay, right? Claudia read the expression on his face. He looked serious. Like he wholeheartedly believed what he was saying. She cut him off. "I can't deal with this right now. My life is a mess, and until I fix things I can't think about being with you or anyone else."

"So that's it. You're giving up on us…on me?"

Claudia turned away and stared intently out the window. The obstacles against them were overwhelming, and just thinking about them—the fraud case, his father, their backgrounds, and the stress of being in a long-distance relationship—caused her temples to throb in pain. "Take care of yourself, Santiago. You're an incredible man, and I wish you nothing but the best."

"This isn't over," he declared, lowering his head and kissing her softly on the lips. "I'll give you the space and time you need, and then I'm going to make you mine."

Chapter 19

"Did you hear me?" Claudia glanced up from her electronic notepad in time to see the head chef squeeze a female server's butt. The celebration bash was in three hours, but the reality TV star was too busy goofing off to listen to her final instructions. He was sampling appetizers, joking with the waiters and dancing to every song that came on the kitchen radio. "I just need five more minutes of your time and then I'll be on my way."

"Relax, Claudia. The extra shipment of crab will be here."

"Today's a big day for the resort," she said. "Everything has to be perfect."

He tossed back a shot of tequila. "I was hoping Santiago's calm, relaxed vibe would rub off on you, but you're still as high-strung as ever."

"I'm not high-strung. I'm organized and efficient and—"

"In need of a good lay!"

At least I don't have the attention span of a toddler, she thought, grinning inwardly. But when Claudia thought about how lonely she'd been all week, and about how much she missed Santiago, her smile faded. She hadn't seen or heard from him since the night she broke up with him, and if she hadn't run into Ana at brunch, she never would have known he'd traveled to Guadalajara for business. He was meeting with architectural genius Warrick Carver to discuss... Claudia couldn't remember. She'd been daydreaming while Ana was chatting and all she knew for sure was that Santiago would be back in time for the celebration bash.

"How are you *really* doing?" Chaz asked, wearing a concerned face. "I heard about the dust-up at the pool party. Are you still mad at Santiago for dumping you?"

Claudia snapped out of her thoughts. "Santiago said *he* dumped *me?*"

"No, the gardener did." He cocked his head to the side and stroked his chin reflectively. "Or was it that hot tamale in housekeeping with the nipple piercing?"

Uninterested in hearing any more resort gossip, she closed her electronic notepad. "I have to check in with the flamethrowers, but if you have any problems just page me."

Chaz followed Claudia out of the kitchen and into the restaurant. "Do you want me to talk to Santiago for you? You know, help smooth things over?"

"No," she said, ignoring the pain she felt at the mention of his name. "We're done."

"Why? Because his dad had too much to drink and insulted you?"

That's putting it mildly. She remembered the scene in Santiago's uncle's backyard—the deadly silence, the stunned faces of the other guests, the contempt in Mr. Medina's tone. To keep from breaking down, she pushed his insults to the furthest corner of her mind.

"You guys are a perfect couple and everyone around here is rooting for you to get back together." He added with a smile,

"Especially Señora Ana! She misses her daughter terribly and having you around has eased some of her pain."

"Did you know Marisol well?"

"No," he said sadly. "I was hired a few months after she passed away."

"I'm doing something special at the celebration bash to honor her memory."

"Really? What is it?"

Claudia told him, and when he cheered, she knew her plan was a winner.

"I hope Santiago and his family like it. The last thing I want to do is—" Claudia stopped when she heard her cell phone ring. She pulled it out of her pocket and put it to her ear. "Hello, this is Claudia Jeffries of Signature Party Planners," she said.

"This is Bert Stimpson from the Richmond Police Department," a raspy male voice said.

Claudia swallowed. Had she been indicted? Was this the beginning of the end?

"I regret having to inform you of this, Ms. Jeffries, but someone broke into your house last night. A neighbor spotted the perps fleeing the residence and immediately called 911."

"Are you sure?" she asked, trying to make sense of what the officer said. "My security company would have contacted me if someone had tripped the alarm."

"You live at 56 Cherokee Road..."

Claudia nodded, though he couldn't see her.

"I'm sorry, ma'am, but there's been no mistake."

"How bad is it?" she asked tentatively. "Is there significant damage to my place?"

"Honestly, it's one of the worst home invasions I've ever seen. It was probably a bunch of neighborhood kids who had nothing better to do, because the whole place was trashed."

Claudia couldn't believe what she was hearing. She couldn't

breathe, couldn't think. It felt like someone was holding her head underwater, pushing her deeper into the dark abyss.

"I was about to head back to the station, but I don't mind hanging around until you get home," the officer said. "We'll need to walk through the house to determine what's missing, and then we'll head down to the station to fill out an official report."

"I'm not in Richmond," she explained. "I'm out of town."

"I can be reached anytime at the police department, so give me a call when you return." Then he hung up.

"Is everything okay?"

"That was the Richmond Police Department…someone broke into my house."

Chaz put his arms around her. "I'm sorry, sweetie. That's terrible."

"I have to…to fly home."

"I'll take you to the airport. Just let me go grab my keys."

"No." Claudia shook her head. "Stay here and make sure things run smoothly."

"Don't worry. I'll take care of everything."

"Tell Ana I'll be in touch." Claudia hustled down the corridor as fast as her sandal-clad feet could take her. And as she dashed past the newly built wedding chapel and into the Oasis Row apartments, she prayed that Santiago would forgive her for breaking her promise. And his heart.

Santiago was blown away.

He'd been to countless parties and had even attended the inauguration ball of the country's former president, but Santiago had never seen anything this grand, this magical. He stood at the entrance of the Bajo La Luna Lounge, drinking in the lively atmosphere. The spacious outdoor lounge was drenched in green, red and white, and the scent of cotton candy filled the air. Guests in sombreros and multicolored beads shook their hips and their maracas to the music the flamenco band was playing on stage. There were pony rides for the kids, boat races for the teens, a photo booth and everything in between. Dozens of people were gathered around a slim redhead cradling a brown capuchin monkey in her arms, and when Santiago saw the jubilant smiles on the children's faces he felt guilty for ever doubting Claudia. She was right, having exotic animals at the celebration bash *was* a crowd-pleaser.

"Tiago, can you believe all of this? It's unlike anything I've ever seen," Ana said, shaking her head. "I feel like a little girl again, and I haven't even gone on a pony ride yet!"

Santiago chuckled. His mom had a Mexican flag painted on one cheek and a flower bouquet painted on the other. Her party hat was sliding off her head, but she was too busy admiring the ice sculpture to notice. An eclectic mix of food, sure to appease even the fussiest eater, was spread out along six buffet tables, and waiters served guests seated in the oceanfront cabanas.

"You're right, Mom. This is pretty spectacular."

"Claudia went above and beyond, and I can't believe how amazing everything turned out." Ana gave her son a one-arm hug. "Did you see the tribute to Marisol?"

Santiago nodded, gazing up at the sky so his mother wouldn't see the sadness in his eyes.

"Your sister would be so proud to see her art displayed in the courtyard. She used to love working outdoors, and she created some of her best paintings right here at the resort."

"It's an amazing exhibit that's been very well-received." Santiago didn't know when or how Claudia put the display together, or where she'd gotten the idea to donate all the proceeds from the exhibit to charity, but he was deeply touched by her thoughtfulness. "My favorite painting is the one she did of you and Dad on your anniversary."

"That's mine too," she admitted, wearing a soft smile. "Your father broke down when he saw it. It's the first time since your sister's funeral that he's shown any emotion, and we both had a good cry as we strode through the rest of the exhibit."

"Are you going to let him back inside the house now?" Santiago concealed a grin. "When I found him sleeping in the office yesterday, I actually felt sorry for him. That couch looks nice, but it's lumpier than a bag of rocks!"

"I was disgusted by the way your father treated Claudia and couldn't stand to be in the same room with him, so I kicked him out," she explained, biting into her macadamia nut cookie. "I think that scared him straight, because yesterday he checked into an outpatient substance abuse program."

"I hope he's finally able to address his issues and quits using alcohol as a crutch."

"Here he comes, Tiago. Be nice." Ana kissed his cheek, then dusted the food crumbs off her hands. "I'll see you later. I'm going to go play Pass the Sombrero!"

Santiago undid the top button of his pinstriped dress shirt and rolled up his sleeves. He was officially off the clock and ready to join in the fun. He picked up a tall glass and poured himself some fruit punch. Keeping an eye out for Claudia, he stood at the lounge entrance, pretending he didn't see his father charging toward him or the wild-eyed expression on his face.

"Where's that Jeffries woman?"

Santiago hit his father with a cold, hard stare. "Why do you want to know? Looking for someone to humiliate?"

"No, I want to hire her!"

"You want to hire Claudia?" he repeated, frowning.

Mr. Medina held up a fat stack of white business cards. "I've received hundreds of inquiries about our guest services department," he explained, his voice filled with excitement. "I just got off the phone with the Crown Prince of Abu Dhabi. The Prince wants to rent out the resort for his fiftieth birthday, and he wants us to plan a week's worth of events for five hundred of his closest friends!"

"Claudia would never work for you," he said, shaking his head. "Not after the way you treated her at Uncle Estevez's pool party."

"Not even if I pay her three times her going rate?"

"It's not about the money," Santiago snapped, gripping his glass. "You humiliated Claudia, and throwing money at her isn't going to make the situation better."

Mr. Medina shrugged. "Maybe you can talk to her for me."

"I'm not letting you come between us again. If she takes me back—" He stopped, cleared his throat, and tried again. "When we get back together, I'm going to show her just how much she means to me, and if that means permanently relocating to Richmond then that's what I'll do."

"Your mom would be devastated."

"Mom can always come visit."

"Do you think it would help if I apologized to Claudia?" he asked, his tone low.

Santiago tasted his drink. "That's a start."

"Sorry to interrupt, gentlemen—" Ramón was panting, and sweat was streaming down his face "—but there's an urgent call for you at the front desk, Santiago."

"Take a message," he said, panning the crowd for his lady love.

"This is the fifth time Ms. Winston's called, and she's become quite hostile."

"Ms. Winston?" Mr. Medina frowned. "Who's that?"

"Señorita Claudia's sister," Ramón explained. "I've paged Señorita Claudia, but she hasn't responded. The bellboy said he saw her rush out of Sueños in tears about an hour ago…"

A growl rumbled deep in Santiago's chest. *I'm going to snap Chaz in two!* "Transfer the call to the kitchen phone," he instructed, marching back inside. "And try paging Claudia again."

"Yes, sir."

Santiago sped into the kitchen, and when he spotted Chaz at the stove, he flew across the room. "What did you do to make Claudia cry?" he demanded, backing the flirtatious chef into the freezer door. "Did you force yourself on her?"

"Me? I didn't do anything!"

"Then why did she leave here in tears?"

"Because she found out her house was vandalized."

A frown creased Santiago's lips. "Who told you this?"

"I was with her when the officer called."

"Where is she now?"

"On her way back to Richmond, I guess." Chaz gave a shrug of his shoulder. "I offered to drive her to the airport, but she turned me down. I bet she's long gone by now."

The phone on the kitchen counter rang. Santiago strode across the room, snatched it up and put it to his ear. "Hello, this is—"

"Forget the pleasantries," a harsh female voice said. "Where the *hell* is my sister?"

Chapter 20

Claudia slid her key into the lock, pushed open the front door and dropped her bags. After countless delays and another three-hour wait in the Dulles International Airport lounge, she was finally home. Broken glass crunched under her feet as she walked through the dimly lit foyer. There was a putrid stench in the air, and when Claudia slapped on the lights and saw the garbage scattered across the floor of her gourmet kitchen, her frustration quickly morphed to anger. Damn kids! Didn't they have anything better to do than vandalize people's homes?

I hope Detective Stimpson gets here soon, she thought, assessing the damage on the main floor. The carpet was stained with muddy boot prints, the dining room chairs were overturned, and there was paper everywhere. She was overcome by emotion, struck down by feelings of despair, but then Claudia remembered Santiago and all the good times they'd shared, and a soft smile touched her lips. Things were up in the air between them, and she didn't know if they'd ever get back together, but she would never ever forget how loved and cherished he'd made her feel.

Claudia heard her cell phone beep and wondered if the new text message was from Santiago. Once she did the walk-through with Detective Stimpson and cleaned the house, she'd give him a call. She owed him an apology for abruptly leaving the celebration bash, and was so desperate to hear his voice she considered phoning him back now—

"Welcome home."

Claudia froze. Shock and denial filled her. A chill shot through her body, and her hands and legs began to shake. *No, no, it can't be!* She glanced to her left, convinced her mind was playing tricks on her—but there, seated on her favorite chair and smoking a cigar, was her ex-husband. He'd lost weight, was sporting a grizzly, unkempt beard, and if not for the pale brown eyes hiding behind rimless designer glasses, she wouldn't have recognized him.

"Since I couldn't come to you, I had to find a way to bring you home," he announced, blowing smoke up into the air. "I knew if something happened to your precious little house you'd come running, so I paid two delightful crooks I met in the county jail to trash the place."

Claudia gathered herself, forced herself to remain calm. She wasn't going to cower away or give her ex-husband the satisfaction of seeing her cry, either. To project confidence, she squared her shoulders, lifted her chin and met his steely gaze. Claudia wasn't the woman she used to be, and she wasn't going to let William intimidate her in her own house. "If you don't leave right now, I'm going to call the police."

"Go ahead." He leaned back in the chair, locked his hands behind his head and propped up his feet. "I'll be right here waiting patiently for you to finish your call."

Claudia wanted to smack his legs off her coffee table, and give him a good, hard cuff upside the head, but she didn't. Instead, she picked up the phone on the end table. It was dead.

Her stomach pitched to the floor, and the fine hairs along the back of her neck shot up.

"Now, where were we?" William raised his index finger above his head. "Yes, right. We were discussing your recent trip to Cabo. I must admit, I was stunned when my informants told me you were screwing Santiago Medina all over his family's resort. You didn't waste any time finding another rich, older man, did you?"

"You had me followed?"

"Of course I did. You have something of great value to me, and I couldn't afford to let anything happen to you while you were in Mexico."

The way he leered at her body made Claudia's skin crawl. He was more cunning than the snake that tricked Eve, a proud white-collar criminal with no conscience. *What did I ever see in him?* she wondered, wishing she could wipe that arrogant smirk off his face. Her cell phone beeped, and an idea struck. Calmly, she slid a hand inside her pocket, felt along the top of her cell phone and pressed the record button.

"I heard you have a meeting with the SEC on Friday," he said, pumping more smoke into the air. "I hope you plan to tell them what a loving husband and generous community leader I was. Because, really, what else is there to say?"

"I'm going to tell them the truth. That you stashed millions of dollars in Swiss bank accounts, used various mistresses to hide money and invested the money you stole in commercial projects."

"Including my wife's event-planning company, Signature Party Planners. Ever consider what will happen to your business when that juicy tidbit is revealed?"

The thought of losing her company made tears sting the back of her eyes, but Claudia didn't crack. "You've destroyed a lot of lives, and all that matters to me is that your victims get the money they invested back. I can always start over. You can't."

He kicked the table clear across the room and surged to his feet. The vase on the coffee table crashed to the floor and shattered into a hundred pieces. "You spoiled, ungrateful bitch," he raged, stalking toward her. "If it wasn't for me you'd be living in your aunt's nasty, rat-infested house, or turning tricks on the corner."

Her heartbeat quickened, racing completely out of control. Winded, as if she'd been kicked in the stomach, she struggled to breathe. Masking her fear, she said firmly, "Get out of my house and don't ever come back."

"With pleasure. Once I retrieve what's mine I'll gladly be on my way." William ripped her purse out of her hand, dumped the contents on the floor, and rifled through her wallet.

"What are you talking about? There's nothing in my bag that belongs to you."

"Oh, yes there is. You just don't know about it." William dug into the billfold, pulled out a blue memory card and kissed it. "I've been looking forward to this day for months!"

Claudia shook her head. "That's not mine."

"I know. I hid it there for safekeeping."

"When? I haven't seen you in over a year."

"I stashed it the day we moved out of Manchester Court. I knew the feds were closing in, so I hid the memory card somewhere they'd never look." He released a deep sigh of contentment as he buttoned his thick, burly coat. "I wish I could stay, but I have a plane to catch."

"You're never going to get away with this."

"Sure I will. Just watch me." William tucked the memory card inside his back pocket. "As you can imagine, the last few months have been incredibly stressful, so I'm heading off to Puangiangi Island for an extended vacation."

Claudia felt her lips part and her mouth fall open. She knew she was gawking, standing there with a wide-eyed expression on her face, but she couldn't believe William was about to jet off to a private island off the coast of New Zealand. Sure, she had recorded their conversation, but what good would it do if the authorities couldn't find him?

"Don't look so surprised." His pale, thin face broke into a broad smile. "You didn't think I was actually going to go to jail, did you?"

William tossed his head back and brayed with laughter.

"I have too much money to ever let that happen. Prison is for stupid people who get caught, and I always stay two steps ahead of the cops."

"I wish we'd never met," Claudia said, wearing a disgusted face. "You're an arrogant, pompous cheat, and you deserve everything that's coming to you."

William grabbed her wrist, gripped it so tight, she felt his fingernails cutting into her flesh. He backed her against the wall and pressed himself roughly against her. He reeked of smoke, and his breath smelled like hot garbage. His gaze was sharper than jagged glass, and a crooked smile appeared on his chapped lips. "I hear you're quite an exhibitionist," he snarled, baring his teeth. "I never pegged you as a closet freak, or the kind of chick who'd give it up on the first date, but my informants tell me you couldn't get enough of your rich Latin lover."

"Let go of me."

"Or what?" he jeered. "It's just you and me, baby. Your sugar daddy isn't here to save you, and evening the score is on the top of my list—"

Something in Claudia snapped. Split in two like a twig. She'd had enough. Enough of people pushing her around, insulting her, calling her names. Smiling sweetly, she raised her leg and threw her knee powerfully into his groin.

Pain sparked in his eyes and flickered across his face. Groaning like a neutered dog, he staggered back into the bookshelf, bounced off the arm of the leather sofa and then fell to the ground like a sack of potatoes. Claudia grabbed a wooden statue off the mantel and raised it high above her head, prepared to strike if William made any sudden moves.

Claudia heard the front door open, the crunch of glass, then loud footsteps on the floor.

"Baby, I'm here now. Everything's going to be okay."

Claudia felt strong arms around her, lifting her off her feet and carrying her across the room and into the kitchen. She inhaled Santiago's scent, and sighed when he whispered words of love and comfort into her ear. The sound of his voice calmed her and made her anger disappear. He held her close, tight, as if he was scared she was going to break free and finish William off.

Two burly Richmond Police officers rushed inside the living room. One handcuffed William, hauled him to his feet and dragged him outside. Detective Stimpson introduced himself and explained how neighbors had spotted William entering the house earlier. Claudia handed over her cell phone, and after recounting what William had said, agreed to come down to the precinct tomorrow to file an official report.

The officer nodded, tipped his hat in her direction and strode out the front door.

Santiago pulled her into the hard ridges of his chest. They stood there for a long moment, drinking in the silence, relishing the joy of being back in each other's arms. Tranquility permeated the air, was so thick around them, Claudia felt high off its fragrance. She couldn't believe that Santiago was here, in Richmond, sitting with her on her black suede couch. Finally, after years of being mistreated and abused, she'd met a man who made her feel loved and protected and whole. *God does care about me,* she thought, clutching Santiago's hands. *He brought this wonderful, selfless man into my life, and I'll never take him for granted.*

"Baby, you're trembling." Santiago stared down at her, a look of concern on his handsome face. "Do you want me to go and get you a blanket? I don't know where your linen closet is, but if you point me in the right direction, I should be able to find it."

"I'm okay. I just want you to hold me."

Santiago brushed his lips across her forehead, drew her closer to him.

"What are you doing here, Santiago? You're supposed to be at the celebration bash."

"No, I'm supposed to be here with you," he stated, his tone matter-of-fact. "And thank God I got here when I did. You would have killed that guy!"

Claudia laughed. She felt invincible, like she could conquer the world. And she would. She had Santiago in her corner, rooting for her, cheering her on, and there was nothing she couldn't do. *I'm going to fulfill my destiny, and nothing's going to stop me.*

"Your sister called the resort looking for you, and after speaking to her I knew I had to come see you," he explained. "I told Chaz to contact the Richmond Police Department and hopped on the Medina family jet."

"You talked to Max? Oh, no. Was she mad?"

"More like livid. I've never heard a pregnant woman use such foul language!"

Claudia wore a wry smile. "I'm sorry. I should have warned you about her. She gets like that sometimes, but her heart is in the right place."

"I told Max I'd take care of everything, and I promised you'd call her later tonight."

"How did things go at the celebration bash?"

"Wonderful. When I left my mom was doing the rumba, and the acrobats were performing their final set. I think you did too good of a job, though. My father wants to hire you!"

Claudia raised her eyebrows. "You're kidding."

"I'm serious, and don't be surprised if Dad calls you tomorrow and begs you to oversee the guest services department for all twelve resorts."

"I won't hold my breath," she quipped. "I feel terrible about missing the party, but I'm thrilled that everyone had a great time."

"And I'm thrilled that we're back together."

"You are, are you?"

Santiago brushed her bangs away from her face. "Claudia, I think about you every minute of the day, and when we're apart my heart aches for you. I won't lose you again, and I'll do anything for us to be together."

His words caused tears to well up in her eyes. Santiago was an esteemed businessman and heir to a multimillion-dollar empire, but he wasn't afraid to be vulnerable with her. And that made Claudia admire him even more. He was a gentle, loving soul, and she felt blessed to have him in her life. "I want us to work, too, Santiago, and I'm completely committed to this relationship. Dating long distance isn't going to be easy, but—"

"I know," he conceded, breaking in. "That's why you're returning to Cabo with me after your meeting with the SEC on Friday."

"Baby, I have a business to run, and employees who are depending on me."

"I know, but I'm confident you can head up our guest services department *and* run Signature Party Planners. And whenever you need to return to Richmond, we'll just hop on my jet," he announced, sporting a giant grin. "Captain Hernandez is an excellent pilot, and his flights are always turbulence-free!"

Claudia smirked. "You've thought of everything, haven't you?"

"Not everything, so let's go into your bedroom and discuss it further…"

"I'm scared to see what it looks like," she confessed, glancing down the hall.

"Then, we'll just have to stay right here."

He rubbed the tip of his nose against her neck, and she giggled.

"Santiago, we can't spend the night in this house. It's filthy, there's no food in the fridge and it reeks of smoke!"

"Paradise to me is wherever you are," he whispered, putting his hand under her chin and turning her face toward him, "and I'm happy as long as we're together. You're the best part of me, and all I care about is loving you for as long as we both shall live."

Claudia said a short prayer of thanks. She'd been angry at God ever since her miscarriage, but as she stared into the eyes of the man she loved, she realized that Santiago had been right all along. They *were* destined to meet. Fate had brought them together to heal and grow, to uncover a deep, all-encompassing love.

"I love you, Santiago."

"Not more than I love you. You're the single most important person in my life, and I can't wait to see what the future holds for us." Santiago put a hand inside his pocket and took out his cell phone. "Which hotel do you want to stay at? I don't care either way as long as—"

"Booking a suite can wait. We have other, more pressing matters to attend to."

"Oh, we do, do we?"

Her eyes sparkled with happiness.

"Well, what exactly do you have in mind?" he asked.

"Enough chitchat," she quipped, straddling his hips and stroking the hard contours of his chest. "I want you to kiss me and you better make it good. I've been waiting all night for this."

Santiago chuckled. "Anything for you, Mrs. Claudia Medina-to-be."

Starting at her neck, he showered light-as-a-feather kisses up to her chin, against her earlobe and across her cheeks. His kisses—the perfect blend of hunger, excitement and desire—

left Claudia feeling breathless, and when their lips finally touched, she moaned her pleasure so loud Santiago prayed her neighbors wouldn't call the cops.

* * * * *

REQUEST YOUR FREE BOOKS!

2 FREE NOVELS
PLUS 2 FREE GIFTS!

KIMANI™
ROMANCE

Love's ultimate destination!

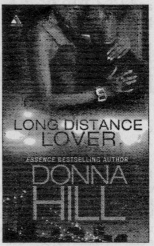